Difficult Times

Joel Loder

Contents

Prologue - Worm of Worlds

A seemingly limitless space of fluffy, brilliant whiteness may be seen. There is no way to surface from this sea of clouds and light. A bright emptiness that glistened in all directions forever, reflecting morning light like the interior of a thick snowbank. This is the Firmament, the erratic sibling of its dismal Abyss cousin.

Despite its beauty, Firmament is extremely harmful because it is high energy proto-matter. The indescribable turmoil that permeates this vast space would throw an unlucky spectator completely out of their environment as their physical form would be torn to shreds and the shreds would be torn to shreds.

The Worm is the only thing that can tolerate exposure to Firmament.

If sound could travel through Firmament, our pitiful observer would in his or her final moments hear a monotonous munch munch sound or even a deep and elastic gorm gorm. the worm's whining as it consumes the Firmament. They regrettably only hear their eardrums rapidly decompressing and their brain's sound-processing centre dissolving into tiny pieces.

It appears as though the Universal Worm is composed of enormous glazed doughnuts. These donuts span an infinite distance when they are piled closely together. The donuts are smallest at the mouth's tip and gradually get bigger as they go along before levelling off and forming a tube-like shape. Its mouth is large enough to swallow staggeringly enormous amounts of material because it is The Universal Worm.

The Worm grows and continues to move mechanically as it consumes Firmament. Watch it advance in a series of jarring waves. The waves come out of the mouth and travel the entire length of the body.

The digestive glands in The Worm's mouth break down each bite of Firmament into its basic constituents, such as earth, air, and water. As a heated, boiling mass, this basic material travels through the intestines.

Watch as The Worm continues to bite, just as it did each of the innumerable times before. As it moves forward, the Firmament comes to life with the sparkling trauma of decomposition, flowing, whirling, and steaming. This bolus might be the beginning of a brand-new world. The components of life as we know it might be present.

However, that remains to be seen. Right now, it's far too hot. Observe the molten earth spewing out damp air. Though it rises away from the surface, it does not disperse but rather gathers into an undeveloped atmosphere.

The gaseous water that will later convert into rain and aid to harden the ground is held in this air. On its way to congregate in lakes and oceans, it will flow through rivulets and streams, sculpting the rugged terrain.

Gravity, a force that is unknown in this universe, appears. The expelled air is kept close to the heavier components. From their intertwined position as Firmament, they are now separated from one another.

Different metals compete for place within the solid lump by differentiating their densities. The cooling mass becomes stratified as they compete for the bottom.

The suns pass as the earth moves along the slippery black intestinal wall of The Worm above the quarrelling minerals and soaring air currents. These internal suns exist A component of its peculiar biology is the Worm. They develop in a line that runs counter to the path the world takes.

A total of 512 glowing yellow circles adorn the figure-eight-shaped course of The Worm's intestine, punctuating the omnipresent night with a few rays of sunlight.

Worlds are made in this manner. Watch as a new mechanism of The Worm enters this brand-new universe, which is round and flat like a coin, filled with seas of ignorance and seeds for mountains, and waiting for the spark of life to settle upon it.

Gods move in to use the virgin material, much like gastrointestinal biota.

Chapter 1 - Undersea Incursion

Everything is repeated eternally elsewhere in an infinite cosmos. However, gods are denied the luxury of infinity within The Worm. They serve as the multiverse pantheon's line cooks. They take what has been implemented on other planes of reality because they need designs that are functional.

Of course, every once in a while a strange god will appear who wants to play with animal parts or who messes around with the reset button. That's acceptable when the pantheon lacks consensus over a course of action or is disinterested in current events. However, you need something sentient to make ends meet, and consciousness begins with a strong foundation of a few resilient creatures in the ocean. No brain exists in a vacuum. They can only thrive in a well preserved global biosphere.

And that is where the narrative begins. in the water. precisely with a hermit crab.

He emerged from a little cave in the living rock where he had been hidden among the coral. This peaceful neighbourhood allowed herbivores, decomposers, and filter feeders to spend time in the sun during the day. The more sedentary creatures were strutting their stuff, the grasses were green, and the fish were vibrant and animated. Clownfish rushed in and out of the polyps' symbiotic homes while they waved their small, seductive tendrils. However, at night, when predators had the upper hand, this proud and vibrant day-life would either go with the sun or risk being hacked to pieces. Without its protective shell, a hermit crab was essentially a grab-and-go meal.

He was jolted back inside when a school of shimmering fish swam by.

The crab had a small diversion from his surroundings thanks to the growth that covered the walls of his hiding place. He carelessly scratched at it to get the scrapes off his pincer. Since the previous peek had been unsuccessful, he needed this more to settle his nerves than for sustenance. He had not seen any open houses. The hunt would go on, therefore he would have to leave the area's relative safety.

Of course, having a place to hide was an excellent idea. It was discreet and little. He might even keep it in mind so that he might return with a good, sturdy shell on his back in the future. A roaming eel or a ravenous octopus wouldn't be deterred by this nook, though, as it was. Any snout-nosed carnivore would also get him right away if it sensed him in the cubby.

The only option left to him was to flee via the open water. He was thinking about a larger snack after nibbling on the wall material, and he had seen a chunk of brown kelp nearby. Despite not being as robust as a coral cubby, this hiding place might nonetheless hold a brand-new dwelling. Kelp was constantly tangled by the tides, usually around a centre of debris. The chances of finding a new home and having a full stomach were equal with a little pincer-grease.

The activity on the reef slowed down. It was now or never.

The crab emerged from his hiding place and leaped out into the sand, which swirled as his spindly legs touched it. He fell softly and slowly. With the aid of his paddle fins, he ran as though on the surface of a small planet. The reef's floor was made up of gentle ridges and slopes that were covered in shifting hypnotic patterns that floated irregularly. The kelp tangle was straight ahead.

He was unaware of the big shadow following him.

The crab leaped off the ground for lengthy glides while paddling frantically. Swimming like way would be hard if he were carrying a large conch or cowrie. His paddle fins would be inside and worthless as propellers, for starters. Unfortunately, it did not provide him an advantage over the viciously skilled hunters with which his species contended during this precarious period between homes. He moved like a stone in the water as opposed to his predators' sleek and agile bodies.

One of these creatures was approaching the unprotected hermit crab and getting ready to strike.

He clutched to the mound while Claw touched some kelp. After only a brief test, he found the kelp to be dense, braided, and without an obvious entry. He then quickly looked about and noticed the monster.

He was about to be attacked by a nurse shark.

Scrambling around the mound's surface, it was ineffective. The strands were unnervingly compact. It would take minutes to cut through them, considerably longer than his remaining life expectancy. Faced with the toothed maw of imminent fate, he mumbled a small grumpy prayer.

The mound began to shift at that point. The crab was covered as it slid over.

The shark veered, becoming abruptly wary.

The kelp tangle displayed a beard by sitting up. In actuality, a gnome awoke from a nap. His attention had been drawn to a loud scrabbling. The crab clung tenaciously to what turned out to be a kelp robe sleeve while yawning and stretching.

Being a race that lives on land, gnomes on the bolas are not known for their skill in the water, but this particular one is an exception. He was recognised by the nurse shark as Amerigo, the reef's keeper and her friend.

She rubbed herself against his side as he held up his arm with a nude hermit crab dangling from it in a weird manner. He rubbed her rough skin and grinned at the interruption, happy to see her, his friend Saethru. She respectfully gave up the quest after he took care of the crab.

Here was a gnome who had given up the accoutrements of society. He was given the resources to live in this submerged hermitage in return for maintaining and guarding the coral community. Now that a creature needed his assistance, he got to work. If this crab was to have any hope of surviving, it needed a place to call home. Amerigo learned the crab's name was Fen and that he was legitimately afraid of exposure through sylvan empathy or by making his own decisions.

The gnome scratched his head and took off his kelp hat, a straightforward conical object made of the same material as his robe. There didn't appear to be any shells nearby, and he didn't have any on him. However, Amerigo was connected.

Because a coral reef is a community, its members are specialised but dependent on one another. The coral itself, which made up the reef's physical structure, served as a filter for dirt and microorganisms as well as a solar energy converter. For instance, the parrotfish would consume the overgrown and decaying coral, destroying too ambitious or underutilised areas of the community. Cleaners, like the numerous tiny prawns and specialised fish, subsisted on the accumulation of daily life. Crevices in the sand were used to build homes. Crabs took the place of little anemone or sponges on their backs as schools taxied swimmers safely through the reefs as a combined effort in mobility and protection.

Everyone was interdependent, cooperating in what appeared to be a chaotic frenzy from the outside but was actually innately orderly and delicately balanced.

Orlith was familiar to Amerigo. That octopus that washes up on the shore would be the perfect host for Fen. Orlith, who lived on the reef's edge, had a propensity to collect intriguing trash as he wandered around the neighbourhood. He also kept the leftovers from his meals. Anything from naturally occurring sand dollars, scallop shells, and crab moults to surface-world artefacts. Unsurprisingly, traces of Amerigo's past are present.

Fen was put under his hat by him. Outside of sight, safe. Some people weren't as polite as Saethru. The group then travelled to Orlith's.

Amerigo moved through the coral's tunnels as one would in their own neighbourhood. The animals initially withdrew in anticipation of Saethru's arrival since they didn't want to make a scene. Amerigo paid no attention, and the general mood started to shift.

They were joined by an angelfish.

A potential wrasse looking to clean followed it.

Others followed, either in an effort to travel more safely in large groups or simply to have a better view of the march. Amerigo soon had a chaotic school accompanying him. The coral labyrinth's eight to twelve foot tall walls rose upward like city skyscrapers. Instead of following the winding trails through the complex, he might have swum high over it to save time and avoid attracting attention. Amerigo, however, preferred to be dressed in tutti-fruity hues. He enjoyed being a part of the limitless life that erupted like a fountain in this tiny island in the middle of the sea.

The novelty of the tour group eventually faded. Each fish ultimately began to pull off as they reached their target or became sidetracked by a lure. Amerigo found the octopus wasn't present when the three got to Orlith's house by themselves.

This would really make it much simpler to loot his collection. He probably wouldn't notice anything missing when he got back from combing, or whatever it was he was out doing. Later, Amerigo could give him a gift, if only to appease his own conscience.

He looked about the house. He couldn't fit through the entrance since it was so little, but he could reach inside all the way to his shoulder. Amerigo began taking items from the floor at random because it was covered in debris. He dug through his pockets and placed an iridescent moon shell, a spiky comb shell, a shattered bottle polished by the sea, a bone smoking pipe, and a gold shoe buckle on the sand next to him.

He placed his cap, which was still holding Fen, on the floor before putting the bottle and shoe buckle back inside, keeping an eye out for a returning octopus. The attractive moon shell, the frightening comb shell, and the finely carved smoking pipe were all that were left.

Fen attempted the pipe after being forced to roll around in the moon shell and being prevented from crawling by the comb shell's spines. Although the stem bounced slightly as he moved, it was useful and sturdy. The bone bowl would protect Fen just as effectively as any shell because it was big enough for him to fit inside.

Fen had located a good place to live. The rejected shells were brought back to the house by Amerigo.

Not wishing to abandon the pipe crab close to the location of an octopus that ate crabs, he considered where to return him when he realised Saethru was not there. He rose over the reef walls while scooping the crab back into his hat for the time being. He possibly could see her from above if she was still in the area. He ascended several feet higher when he crested the coral walls. The water's surface felt near, but he could make out the reef in front of him, a chaotic mix of vibrant, struggling organisms.

He didn't find any nurse sharks, but he did spot two unfamiliar figures. They were hanging out together in the reef and were a deep, dark blue colour. They were at least double his size. It was hard to judge from a distance. To avoid being seen against the surface light, he descended.

He cautiously made his way back to the coral trench, creeping up to bends and being ready to conceal in case somebody appeared out of nowhere. The locals sensed something new because the activity from their earlier tour across the reef had died down. Amerigo observed a sea floor covered in debris. The crushed coral was sprinkled with an uprooted anemone. Similar evidence of devastation became more frequent as he continued.

He eventually came across them and hastily retreated to remain hidden. Two merpeople were standing nearby. They weren't much bigger than Amerigo, though. Their gnome-like torsos, fishy heads, and characteristic finned tails were all covered in dark blue scales.

The sand behind him was stirring. Amerigo froze as it wiggled between the space between the coral and the surface.

When the cloud cleared, Saethru was back by his side.

She had remained hidden in a small alcove, probably just as upset as the rest of the reef by these invaders. She was resolved to rejoin him when he passed where she was hiding. Amerigo patted his friend while sighing. It gave him a thought.

Amerigo skulked back the way he came and checked on the inhabitants of the reef. Many were hesitant to follow him. When he said he wanted to fight these alien characters, they backed off. He occasionally discovered willing combatants, who he led to the appropriate locations. One of these slithered up his robe's sleeve.

Saethru responded to Amerigo's complex gesture by departing to complete her own task. Now he could go back and observe the two amusing wrecking balls as he awaited a chance to dispatch them.

However, the two were absent.

While Amerigo's back was turned, they went on. He moved cautiously towards where they had gathered just moments ago in the hopes of discovering a clue. One of the sponges they had been poking to death was there, on the coral wall. It was hanging in distressed shreds and clung to the base. He silently cursed these tourists while holding the torn object.

Over him, a shadow descended. The two merpeople were approaching when he turned around.

One had a hook that punctured its fishy lip and was larger than the other. It appeared to be deliberately morbid. The other had crisscrossing scars down his slender forearm and was emaciated in comparison.

Fish that were stuck to the pike like receipts on a desk spike were carried by the hook-mouth. Some wriggled ineffectively. Amerigo's hand lunged as the merpeople peered over his shoulder, causing the coral to fall. He pulled out something Amerigo couldn't see and stacked it on top of the rest of his weapon. a tang of yellow.

Amerigo withdrew towards the wall as the coral dust covered him and the two goons grinned at him with their flat eyes.

Net-bound attempted to touch Amerigo's shoulder but backed away.

His kelp robe's neck unfolded a black and white ring that looked like a sea snake with a lot of poison. Net-bound sputtered and ducked behind his larger partner, who grinned.

The merfolk were more physically robust, better suited for swimming, and larger. Unavoidable fact, really. As well, none of those three things stood alone as the sole determinant of success on the reef. Amerigo leaped off the wall as Hook-mouth handled a trembling Net-bound. He gained a brief advantage, but as he round the corner, a Hook-mouth was right behind him, closely followed by a cautious Net-bound.

His energetic tail darted past the curve as he dove down a side lane. He continued along this path until he encountered a fork.

Hook-mouth in front of him blocked his attempt to turn right. Not as stupid as he appeared to be. In order to capture him at the outflow later on, the merfolk had rushed by.

Amerigo turned around and saw Net-bound heading in the opposite direction, coiling and weaving, nearly loping. He appeared eager to catch up but wary of the snake that was still attached to Amerigo.

Before one of them could get to him, he took the left branch of the fork.

But it was useless. This came to a stop in a dead end.

Hook-mouth was grinning once more as they closed the gap, trapping the gnome. He moved steadily and confidently with his pike ready to spring if Amerigo did anything. The net-bound, who was becoming increasingly unsteady, jittered behind the larger merpeople.

They came to a stop a few feet away, the larger of the two clearly agitated by his hesitant partner. He turned and made a tight fist with Net-bound's arm. The smaller merfolk trembled and ceased jumping around nervously.

Hook-mouth pushed Net-bound forward while smoothly pressing the pike's shaft into his hand. Amerigo saw and understood that this terrified person was now in control of his life. He held the wavering point out and sculled carefully forward, just giving the stern Hook-mouth a quick glance in the rear.

Amerigo's sleeve let forth a black-and-white tendril, and he grabbed the sea serpent and raised it to aim towards the frail merpeople. Despite the distance being quite a few feet, he retreated once more, practically backing into Hook-mouth.

He pushed a Net-bound who was resisting ahead while rolling his eyes once more. The three of them remained there for a short while, taking care to avoid the spark that would set the keg on fire. Net-bound followed Amerigo's downward-flicking glance after his eyes. Directly beneath the unaware merpeople, a gaping maw opened like a burlap sack. Net-bound's tail was drawn in by a living bear trap that Amerigo had recruited: a frogfish. The merfolk, which usually smothers rather than dismembers its prey, was too small to fit inside.

When Net-bound saw his steadfast partner again, he turned to him again and yanked at him while flailing around in a state of hysterical panic. Like a pitbull, the frogfish was clinging. Amerigo seized the chance to swim out of the ditch and upstream. With a contemptuous expression, Hook-mouth grasped the pike in his hands and freed himself. He left Net-bound to fend for himself as he set off in pursuit of the gnome.

The merfolk were catching up to the gnome as they skimmed across the coral's surface. Even with years of practise, thrashing with four limbs couldn't compete with a strong fishtail. It pushed the pike ahead through the water while getting in closer proximity to the gnome's kicking and paddling. He made an ever-increasing number of unsuccessful attempts to elude a vengeance homing torpedo.

Hook-mouth was then suddenly tackled from the side. Saethru had been observing from above, poised to shoot with a swift, direct blow. The creature was knocked into a fire coral even though she missed the grip with her jaws. He was stung by polyps like a beehive.

Amerigo turned around to observe the outcome. The merfolk writhed, seeking to free himself from the paralysing venom, but was only able to drag fresh skin across the stingers as Saethru sped off for another round. Despite not being fatal, Amerigo was familiar with the fire coral's potential for excruciating pain.

Net-bound climbed the wall's ledge on all fours. He sent the frogfish flipping end over end with one last flick, but it quickly righted itself and swam away. After spotting his friend, the merfolk moved towards them and lifted the larger Hook-mouth onto his shoulders. He turned and swam off after barely pausing to give Amerigo a deathly stare.

He lured the snake out of his robe and sent Saethru after them, warning him of their reversal. They had earned a reward, but Amerigo only had the crab he had recently adopted on him. The snake deserved something, though.

He observed the pike that the merpeople had left behind. When he examined it, the skewered fish were all long gone, so he began taking them out. He would use a stone to anchor each fish as he removed it to the ground. Most likely, the snake wouldn't eat them all, but some sort of scavenger would pass by and find a free lunch.

He discovered there was one more item fastened to the pike after the last fish was taken out. There was a stone talisman with the head of a trident in front of a net background that was tied on with string. While waiting for Saethru to return, he took it out of the weapon and studied it. Even though it was obvious that the merfolk were completely retreated, something didn't seem right. In order to avoid the drop-off, they had run north. outside of their house.

He quickly made his way to the one person who could provide him additional information about these thugs after taking the talisman.

****

The ritual used to make contact with a deity is greatly influenced by that deity. The deity of the sea and storms, Contacting Stormhaegen, had specific provisions for his followers, who frequently resided on, near, or even under water. Stormhaegen veered away from what Deos, the god of magic and artifice, could need—candles and a steady drawing hand—and what Neos, the god of the hearth and community, might need—a stocked pantry and a bustling dining hall. He really preferred a spot where he could converse comfortably and some insignificant object to hold his attention.

Saethru was instructed to wait outside the overgrown coral temple by Amerigo. She was a nurse shark, which meant that she had unique adaptations that allowed her to pour water over her gills, allowing her to breathe without constantly moving. She focused on that while hiding in the sand.

He proceeded past the threshold to the straightforward cairn that served as his god's altar. It was a warm, cheerful setting. The hermitage's altar's affable simplicity served as its main draw. After placing the token on the altar, Amerigo started to think.

Luminous plasma emitted from coral spines and plant tips glittered in the atmosphere. Amerigo let out a tiny sigh of relief. His scattered thoughts kept returning to his meeting with the merpeople. Normally meticulous, Stormhaegen could easily dissuade the deity from appearing with such a scatterbrained mind. It appeared like he was open to speaking today.

Against all known laws of meteorology, a cloud developed underwater amid the dancing, crawling sparks. Large and loud, with booming giggles that filled the area like rolling thunder and an ear-to-ear smile on his beard, a guy emerged from the nimbus. He showed up wearing a bathrobe that was blue in colour and had elaborately detailed shimmering patterns on it. He had the appearance of a bigger, rounder gnome.

Instead of hair, he had clouds hanging over his face. Straight wispy stratus at the top, with fluffy cumulus for a beard and chest hair that sprang out where the bathrobe closed.

The god exclaimed, "Welcome Amerigo! It feels like ages since you visited my shrine! busy as usual tending to the garden. One day, we should take a stroll there! I haven't physically manifested here in a very long time, and I'd really like to witness its beauty in person! You did a good job! Do you have anything to share with me?

The god was speaking incoherently, oblivious to Amerigo's frantic motions for haste, which the god had only recently observed.

He leaned over his nimbus and inquired, "What is that you have there?"

The stone talisman left behind by the earlier merpeople had been manufactured by Amerigo. The storm god gave it some thought. He examined the token for a brief while before casually reclining and waving it away.

"Yes, yes, the incursion on my beloved reef," he remarked in the voice of a man entrusted with reporting negligent neighbours. With a wave of his palm, he created a small landscape out of swirling clouds. Some places were recognisable to Amerigo. Dark, furious clouds, for instance, showed the southern decline. These stood in stark contrast to the reefs he looked after, which were depicted in the morning's technicolour sherbet.

The chart shifted as he watched, mimicking the passage of a storm front. Dark clouds attempted to suffocate the vibrant colours by creeping up and over the sherbet like an amoeba. Amerigo grew pallid.

"I am aware of it. It is a problem. But you shouldn't worry, Amerigo. I'm glad you came to me since I have a strategy to deal with these intruders. The god relaxed in his cushioned couch and patted his tummy.

Amerigo appeared relieved.

As if reading the interior of his eyelids, Stormhaegen talked while his eyes were closed.

He murmured, "The portents are...vague," loud enough that Amerigo felt someone listening at the water's surface may hear him. The god instructed Amerigo, in what might have come off as a faux mystical tone if he had not known him better, "You must find...a filthy lizard. His...queenly aura will help you identify him. As he spoke, he waved his fingers in front of him.

He looked up and shook his head.

"Totally absurd to me."

Amerigo sank.

But on this issue, it's obvious. This chosen one is expected to bring about whatever is necessary and eliminate the merfolk threat at its root. He continued to wave his hands indefinitely before speaking in an assured manner.

Amerigo acted normally around Stormhaegen, masking his confusion beneath a stern expression of responsibility.

Stormhaegen commanded regally, "Go where I send thee, to the bleak northern wastes. I have planned a quick but affordable mode of transportation. No need to say thanks.

Amerigo appeared startled. He was genuinely terrified when he was propelled through the air and out of the water.

The struggling devotee swiftly walked away from the altar against his will while the sea deity calmly observed with resolve.

Travel via air. Stormhaegen said the phrase "transportation of the gods" to no one in particular.

Chapter 2 - Chicken Soup

The gods of the bolus lived in a state apart from the physical. For those who do not comprehend the deific waveform of reality, it could be described as an apartment. In this apartment, a man with the head of an eagle sat on something here represented as a couch, his feet up on an ottoman, lazily watching images on what was in essence a TV. Behind the eagle-headed god, whose name was Outeb, was the analog of a kitchen table, on which were two mouse-sized mice, white of fur and clad in robes. They were busy coordinating a full-sized quill to write on a piece of parchment.

Stormhaegan stormed in, as only a storm god can, turning the atmosphere tumultuous.

"I'm back from my walk!" he proclaimed. "Don't bother getting up, Outeb, I can see you're comfortable."

Stormhaegen skirted the bird-headed god of travel to sit on the far side of the couch. He waved a hand at the screen across from them purposefully. The image changed.

"I have urgent business," Stormhaegan said hastily to his couch companion. "I hope you don't mind."

"Urgent business?" a voice squeaked. It didn't come from the vegetative deity. One of the mice had squoken. "Are you finally doing something about my prophesy?" it asked scornfully, "The one at the top of your To Do for a millennium now?"

The images on the screen rapidly shifted as Stormhaegan flicked them by, barely allowing each to register. "Yes, your damned list. I said I would get around to it."

The mouse huffed and returned to its scribbling. "It's a miracle the world hasn't drowned yet. Or frozen."

"Or melted," the other mouse added. Outeb watched in stony silence, his beak partly open like an avian filter feeder. Stormhaegen grew impatient, his cosmic power limited by simple disorganization.

"Aha!" he announced. He nudged Outeb and said, "Great advice on the air travel. Missionaries, tactically deployed. Scribb? What am I looking at?"

"It was in the prophesy I wrote for you," said one of the mice.

"I couldn't read your handwriting. Footprints were all in the ink."

The scratch of quill on parchment stopped, replaced with a tense silence. This faded and was followed by a squeaky sigh. "Let me come over there. I'll walk you through it."

They scurried to the TV and climbed up to the screen. The two mice studied the moving picture, a sunny desert vista overlooking a great clay cooking pot, a small ugly humanoid in a chef's hat dancing on an adjacent mezzanine. A reptilian humanoid, its hands bound, was secured nearby.

"That's him," one of the mice confirmed. "Your chosen one."

"That thing in the hat is a kobold?"

A mouse shook its head. "The other one is a kobold."

Stormhaegen panicked.

"I'm too late! Those goblins are going to eat him!"

"No, no," one of the mice said, "This is now. When did you send your herald, his guide?"

Stormhaegen scratched his scalp, stirring the clouds there.

"Oh... Yesterday?"

"Then we need to get you caught up. We can squeeze a day's recap in the few minutes of real time until he makes his appearance."

The scene on the TV started moving backwards.

****

While a gnome and a hermit crab hunted for shells, millions of other things were happening at the same time. There is nothing particularly unusual or noteworthy about this, as millions of things tend to happen simultaneously all the time. For instance, two snails fell in love after a chance meeting while crawling over a garden pumpkin. A convict was wrongly hanged in front of a jeering crowd. A priceless vase was smashed. A stoic achieved enlightenment, the result of years of study. Someone fended off an attacker using a priceless vase which happened to be at hand.

Few of these things are directly related, with most of them being separated by vast distances. They just happened at the same time, and it's comforting to know that when one thing is happening, millions of other things are happening right alongside it in a great chaotic orchestra. And one of those, far away from the gnome and hermit crab, was a kobold exploring the desert in which he lived.

A kobold, in appearance, is a small, savage lizard which has learned the twin tricks of using tools and walking upright. These two things are the unspoken cost of admission the civil discourse. The civil discourse is like a game. Rules are settled on by committees, which are then put to the test by the players, to the amusement of onlookers who often have some investment in who comes out on top. This leads to further discussion about who hit whom, whether they stepped over the line or not, and inevitable accusations of cheating. These lead to re-evaluation and more rules, and the cycle begins anew. But kobolds choose instead to watch the game from a nearby hill. There may be no popcorn, but they can eat as many bugs as they can catch. They are, however, sometimes hit in the head by the occasional fly ball.

The kobold race populates the wastelands east of the mountains. Here they organize into tribes, which they fiercely protect. Your average kobold is roughly half the height of an adult orc which, luckily, is often just tall enough to reach the ground. This is excepting a kobold named Punig, who was allegedly so short he needed something to stand on just to get up in the morning. They also come in a variety of stone- and metallic-colors, their scales being a homogenous hue.

This kobold is named Chicken, in the language of his people, and he is away many days searching for the bounty of the land. Chicken is unconcerned with astronomy, philosophy, and what the civilized world calls "the natural magics." The world to him consists mostly of the territories he patrols, those being only a small portion of the greater vast and hostile wasteland.

The wastes do not take readily to being tamed and scoff openly at the thought of being cultivated, so the kobolds and some of its other denizens have adopted a strategy of subsistence scavenging. The tactic consists of searching far and often for anything edible or practical. Moderately experienced with this style of living, Chicken has an established route. Going solo, as opposed to joining the rare hunting party in search of big game, there are a few places he knows to check for goods.

He doesn't have much room in his pack, but this is of little import. Naturally curious, Chicken brings back information, whether rooted out of cracks or picked up like a stone on the side of the path. It weighs nothing and there's always room for more.

He checks in with the migratory beasts, notes the weather, and scouts the boundaries of rival tribes, kobold or otherwise. Kobolds, collectively, are territorial in a righteously indignant way, to other kobolds and to non-kobolds alike. News of encroaching tribes could spark war parties. Really big encroaching tribes could spark an intense and immediate urge to pack up and move. None are too righteous or indignant to risk suicide.

In the same vein, Chicken is also interested in finding places to hide, though this information he keeps to himself. A hiding spot is no good if others know where it is. Some of Chicken's forays last for days, and he does not like being exposed to the elements in the dark. Some elements have teeth, powerful jaws, and a knack for moving silently.

When he finds an interesting structure to the rocks, he has made it a habit to investigate no matter the time of day, because it could be useful in the future.

He found one such structure presently, and was wriggling inside the space as cautiously as could be managed. A mere slit in the shattered ground, it was well hidden, being small and interestingly angled. It appeared to comfortably house anything that could fit through the opening. Chicken was testing if he measured up. He had already set aside his pack, removed the stone knife hanging from his waist, and glanced around suspiciously before making the attempt. It was quiet now, but Chicken knew he couldn't trust the silence further than he could throw it.

The bassy scent of the basalt and quartz accented the omnipresent sandstone dust and desiccated dung as the hot air carried it skyward. Chicken lay half in the hole, half out of it. It stubbornly refused admittance to both halves at once, so he took a moment to rest. He had a piece of charcoal in hand and was marking this new place. Two triangles, touching at opposite points, crossed by a line. Two legs, two arms, a tail, and a distinctly kobold-looking head in profile. It was just a way of saying "Chicken was here". Satisfied, he returned to fighting the hole.

Half into the twisted about. He tried to come in straight, and then at an angle, all while pulling with his arms and pushing with his legs. His tail curled with the effort as the narrow opening squeezed his chest and the rough stone abraded his scales and tunic.

This last detail went largely unnoticed as kobold scales are particularly tough, much more-so than common lizardfolk scales. In the few circles where these things are discussed, kobold scale toughness is attributed to a thickening over generations, as only kobolds with thick scales survive the rigors of their environment to mating age. This is patently wrong

His color, however, was selected for. To better blend into his environment, Chicken is covered in an overlapping natural mail of goldenrod colored scales. These scales cover him head to toe, from the tip of his triceratops frill down to his short-clawed toes and the tip of his tail.

Accenting this was the slightly lighter color of the scales on the front of his torso and palms, his stubby crest horns, and the claws on his hands and feet.

The tunic he was wearing, and absentmindedly destroying against the rocks, was cut of a salvaged canvas cloth and lined with fur. The lining was done inexpertly, but clearly with purpose.

Frustrated, he pulled his upper half out of the hole and frowned at it.

"I know I can fit. You're going to let me in, even if I have to force you," he said to the obstinate just-too-small hidey hole. It merely gaped at him.

He picked up a comfortably shaped rock and started to widen the hole with it, pounding against the most offending parts to smooth them down. After several minutes, sending chips of stone flying, he brushed away a poke in his side and set his rock down to try again to enter the hole.

There was another poke in his side before he could get his head in.

Behind him were two curious goblins, one of which was using a blunted dagger tied to a pole as part-time spear, part-time pokey stick. They had been watching him with idle bemusement, barely having to sneak up on him in his severely focused state.

"Oh, hello," he said, grinning nervously. "I wasn't supposed to see any goblins until tomorrow. You don't think you can let me off with a warning, do you?"

After a brief scuffle, Chicken reflected on how the sound of his banging must have attracted them. The goblins dragged him away with his arms bound uncomfortably in thick twine.

The pair spoke frantically to each other in gobbledygook along the way. Once, they turned their attention on Chicken, spitting foul gibberish at him, making him wish they'd just hurl stones instead. Gobbledygook, the language of the goblins, is the most unpleasant language spoken on the bolus, often compared to the experience of pouring acid in the ears. The blank stare won from him after the verbal assault told them that Chicken didn't grok the language.

The first chance he got, Chicken tried to get the rope between his teeth, but the goblins noticed and shouted at him. After that, the troop did not stop until they reached their destination, which was just before nightfall. Chicken could see a crude fence corralling boulders. These boulders had obvious signs of habitation strung between them.

"Do you smell smoke?" Chicken asked, "I think I can smell cooking from here." The goblins didn't hear, or didn't care.

The group had, in fact, arrived at the goblin camp.

His captors shouted and gibbered at a perimeter guard before heading on past the tall and spikey fence and deeper into the goblin camp.

I don't like the look of those skulls, Chicken thought to himself as they passed through the open gate. They hung from the posts like large white grapes, clustered and sun bleached, in random assortments of race.

There were few structures inside the perimeter, with most of the goblins sleeping or loitering guiltily among the boulders. If they weren't loitering, they hustled about with a nervous energy.

Chicken could hear talking, or maybe fighting, going on around him. It was hard to tell the difference.

There were a few lean-tos here and there. At the center of the fenced in area stood a full-sized leather tent, but even this was dwarfed half again by the great clay pot next door.

There was scaffolding around the pot for someone to get to the top, and it was propped up over a roaring bonfire. This bonfire was pulling double-duty to also light most of the camp.

Chicken gawked at the size of the fire and noticed that the activity going on was largely focused on gathering fuel. He couldn't see a goblin not carrying something dry and flammable. He watched a few huck their load into the flames before turning around and trotting off for more.

He realized with dread that this pot was where his captors were taking him.

They surprised him by stopping him at the tent first, whereupon another goblin emerged with much pomp, given the circumstance.

Casting aside the tent flap, this goblin gave Chicken an appraisal like a fashionista would give someone wearing last year's clothes. He felt like a squished bug under this goblin's regal and judgmental gaze.

Clearly outclassed by this arrival, his guards jabbered nervously, a stark contrast to the belittling tone they had given the perimeter guard.

The regal goblin wore the nicest of scrap clothing, with a chef's hat featuring prominently on his head, giving him an extra foot of height. The poof at the top was level with Chicken's eyes.

Chicken mustered his guile.

"Thank the gods," he said, his voice petulant and filled with entitlement, "Finally, someone in charge here. Listen, there has been a big misunderstanding."

He envisioned himself as a bereaved chieftain as he spoke, supplementing his confidence.

He switched to a more complacent tone, with a sense of bargaining in his words.

"If you let me go now, there will be no repercussions. We can look back on this and laugh."

The guards, unfazed by his act, cut his chuckle short by pulling him down to his knees with an "oof", killing the moment.

He looked the goblin in the face, yellow eye to yellow eye. He expected the goblin to reach out and move his head side to side, but all it did was lean in and sniff deeply. The head chef yammered decisively and both guards acknowledged. Chicken would do for the occasion. He was goblin handled up the rickety scaffolding, restrained through his thrashing.

"No! Please! You don't want to eat me! I'm not very tasty!" he shouted, all composure lost.

The goblin had already gone back inside, dismissing the issue. From up on the adjacent landing, Chicken could see into the bubbling brew. It was grey with swirling wisps of green, like rusty mercury, and occasionally an eyeball or piece of chitin or some gizzard or such would bob to the surface. The smell of the tincture climbed in his nostrils and settled in, watering his eyes and making him gag.

Chicken had once come across the carcass of a coyote in a sealed crevice after a rockslide, the creature having succumbed to a broken back after some time. It had died in the relative cool of a watering hole, and instead of desiccating in the sun, it served as food source for the tenacious fungus which grew there. The damp, dead air of that coyote's tomb, unearthly and sickly with the accelerated decay caused by the culture of fungus was a smell Chicken would never forget. That smell was this smell's younger brother. With a hint of chicory.

A whack to the back of his legs told him his captors wanted him to sit, which he did, and they tied his already bound hands to a pole jutting from the slapdash.

"You're not throwing me in there yet?" he asked hopefully, but then added, "Maybe you want to chop me into pieces first. Though to do that you'd have to descale me, I guess. I dunno, really, I've never eaten kobold, myself." His train of thought ended with a pitiful shrug. "I've got them right where I want them. Everyone knows the hero always escapes the cannibals when they've got him spitted over a fire. I just need my trusty blade."

He realized he had no trusty blade.

"My loyal sidekick will come through for me, at least."

No one came to mind.

"My legend simply can't end before it started. I'll keep my mind off it until my daring escape."

All night long, Chicken's mind wandered in and around unpleasant thoughts while he waited to be made into Chicken soup.

Chapter 3 - Expeditious Miracle

Dawn crept over the horizon. In its wake, pitch black changed to greys, and greys changed to color, bringing a new day. A day that, on a cosmic level, was functionally identical to the one before. The word "cosmic" here is generally used for its definition "pertaining to, or containing, worms." A gardener may attribute the success of his prize winning zucchinis to his cosmic soil, or may be told by an equally disgusted and medically fascinated doctor of his cosmic bladder. This is all to say, the worms would never know a new day had dawned.

Chicken woke up, having not realized he had slept. Things were now happening in the goblin camp, and he found he had not made a daring escape overnight and was still tied to a pole next to a giant bubbling pot. He was sore in many places, having been denied simple comforts like bed clothes, room service, and freedom of movement.

A procession of goblins was approaching the scaffolding in an almost reverent procession. Armed goblins with grim faces led the way for what looked like robed individuals.

Among them was a frail and saggy goblin, wrapped in a scrap of cloth like a shawl, who was moving in a way more comfortable than quick. It was attended by the several robed goblins. They were helping support the old and teetering thing, keeping it from keeling over dead, which looked more likely with every step.

The smell from the pot was making Chicken woozy. Breathing it all night made his throat and sinuses feel like they were coated in algae slime.

Several eons later, the procession reached the mezzanine, at the top of which Chicken was tied to his pole. They at least didn't hurry the old goblin.

It was hard for Chicken to read their stony grim faces, so he spectated, idly wondering who this goblin was. There wasn't much else for him to do, and it got his mind off the boiling pot sitting just below the edge on the other side from the procession.

When they reached the top, the guards checked and double-checked Chicken's bonds. An attendant placed a seat, a short wooden tripod stool, on the other side of the platform from him.

"I'm surprised you don't creak when you bend," Chicken muttered as the old goblin sat down.

"I lucky to have reached old age," it said in a voice like cobwebs and rust, "unlike you. I live full longly. It makes me happy."

Startled, Chicken forgot to process the garbled words. It had spoken to him in his own language.

While he played them back in his mind, the goblin continued, "I happy to contribute to goblin tribe. It the least I can do." It sounded mournful.

Chicken regained his footing, so to speak.

"If you can speak my language and gobbledygook, you can tell them to let me go," Chicken said, now fully caught up. "I'm not tasty boiled. I don't meet the qualifications for a roast."

There was a popping and creaking noise. What Chicken had thought was the stool rocking under the old goblin was in fact laughter.

"No, no," it said eventually, "Gobbos no make mistake. You sacrifice. You get to be part of goblin boil, just like I."

Before he could elaborate further, a hooting noise started down below. Chicken noticed there were no more goblins in the distance bringing fuel to the fire. They were all gathered around the pot, looking expectantly at the chef goblin's tent.

With a smart flip, the tent flap was cast back and the head chef appeared.

It stepped out majestically and the crowd cheered. The chef goblin held its hands up for a moment and soaked in the praise, then ducked back into the tent, quieting the crowd. Making another entrance, it came back out to even more raucous approval, holding a great brown mushroom aloft.

Chicken could only just hear the quiet old goblin over the crowd.

"Secret ingredient for goblin boil. Make it special. Make it goblin boil."

Chicken realized the old goblin was talking about the mushroom the chef goblin was holding, staring at it as though enamored by the fungus.

****

Amerigo had been flying for hours.

The bubble of sea water in which he was suspended had been soaring at speed the entire time.

He hadn't screamed at first, having lived his life in silence since becoming the reef caretaker. It wasn't first nature to him any more. Fen, having no vocal cords, couldn't scream, but he was digging into Amerigo's scalp with each leg and claw.

There was no sensation of wind, just of unearthly movement.

By now, there was nothing left for Amerigo to empty from his stomach, though its attempts at trying again were coming at longer intervals. The water was disconcertingly cloudy.

The back of his mind, Amerigo's calm center, calculated that his trajectory had leveled out, and only now was the bubble starting to return to the ground.

Just not in so many words.

Today's sun was rising over the edge of the world to his right, pink-ening the clouds and blue-ening the sky.

Some said the world was flat, and having seen it at this height, Amerigo could believe them. The horizon stretched out in a straight line in both directions, disturbed only by the large forma-tions which dotted the wastes.

The sun, those same people said, was different every day of the year, with each passing over the earth in turn. Supposedly they were a kind of bioluminescence, like what some denizens over the drop off employed, designed to foster life on worlds which passed through the digestive tract of a giant worm. But a digestive tract that recursed on itself. One complete pass through the cycle marked a year. Diagrams in textbooks show what the academics long deliberated, measured, and attempted to disprove.

The tract was a figure-eight. The straight-aways, with no bend in the curve, were short intermediary parts of the year, spring and fall. Either end of the figure-eight, the world and suns swapped the inner track. With the suns on the inside of the curve, they were spaced further apart, allowing the nights to be longer and to cool the bolus, enacting winter. With the bolus on the inner track, the suns are angled such that the rays converge more closely, shortening the night and overall heating the bolus. This is their summer.

And this is one story among many told to explain the change in seasons and the course of the year. This one has the benefit of being true.

Stormhaegen offered no insight, and required no doctrine, regarding any one belief about the physical nature of the universe, so Amerigo was free to speculate at his leisure.

Right now, as his stomach tried to turn itself inside out again, he had decided the universe was simply too big, too fast, and too much.

****

The head chef climbed the scaffolding much more nimbly than the old goblin did. He was practically dancing, swinging at the switchbacks, and trying to stay in the view of his adoring public.

The crowd exploded again when he made it to the top.

He moved from one side of the platform to the other, playing the crowd, getting each side to out-scream the other by waving the mushroom around.

Chicken noticed a sharp metal knife dangling from the chef's belt, the only untarnished metal he'd seen since he had arrived.

At a gesture from the head chef, the crowd quieted to half their enthusiasm.

It was just enough for the chef to shout over them, launching into his monologue for the occasion. Unfortunately for Chicken, he spoke in gobbledygook.

"Chef say, today is momentous day," the old goblin translated, "Today is day of goblin boil."

Its expression was one not of helpfulness, but one that sought to torture Chicken. The chef shot a glance at the interruption, displeased, but clearly unwilling or unable to stop the old goblin.

Chicken tilted his head at the goblin playing the crowd.

"Chief? He's your chief?"

The old goblin shook its head vigorously.

"No! Chef! Chef!"

It pointed to its own bald head. Chicken looked back at the chef hat on the other one's head.

"And what are you?" Chicken hissed at him. "Are you one of their priests, here to bless the meal or something?"

The creaking sound again. It found Chicken's plight funny. The chef's monologue continued over the slight noise.

"No, no. I sacrifice too. You, me. Sacrifice. Important for goblin boil."

The chef hit a beat in his speech. He gestured respectfully to the old goblin, who stood at the cue. The attendants had returned as if out of the air, Chicken not noticing their arrival in the confusion. One had affixed a ramp leading down to the lip of the pot. A short pier over pungent bubbling muck.

The chef and attendants were suddenly more reserved, bowing respectfully to the aged goblin.

"It is time," it said turning back to Chicken, "I sacrifice. I happy to go. See soon, other sacrifice!"

It was disrobed and helped willingly into the goo, its face locked in a peaceful expression as it sunk below what had to be scalding liquid. The fire had gone through the night, the hot liquid keeping him warm through his imprisonment.

Chicken's mouth went dry.

The old goblin did not come back up.

After a few moments, the crowd decided it was time to cheer again, and the chef switched back to his previous stage-drunk attitude.

He bounded over to Chicken and leaned over him. With a crisp sliding sound, he produced his knife. Looking him in the eye, he gabbled something indecipherable only to Chicken.

Though fearing for his life, Chicken could only reply with a confused, "...what?"

Apparently satisfied, the chef hopped over to the pot again, tempting danger by skipping right up to the edge of the ramp.

Holding the mushroom and knife aloft, he finally concluded his monologue, emphasizing the last three syllables and igniting the crowd yet again.

He started to chop the mushroom in his hand.

But before the first cut, he froze like a statue.

The crowd hushed, waiting for what outlandish bit of showman-ship he was going to spring on them in these final moments. In the silence, there was a light keening sound, previously unheard behind the cheers.

It was growing louder.

The crowd looked around anxiously, everyone trying to find the source. It was coming from everywhere at once. Chicken heard someone shout "Gobbedygoo!" and saw a member of the crowd pointing up.

He followed the finger and saw, coming in fast from above, the world's biggest raindrop.

And it was screaming.

****

The ground was coming close fast.

Below him, Amerigo could see a crowd of ants in a semi-circle around a fire with a tiny pot over it.

The scene was rapidly growing beneath him, filling him with a fresh new panic.

He suddenly realized he'd been screaming again.

The ants became more distinct, but unrecognizable. The tooth-pick structure grew into one apparently made of logs.

The pot grew from a thimble, to a campfire pot, to something the size of a temple bell.

No matter how he flailed, Amerigo was stuck flying face first towards-

****

Chicken braced for impact while the chef stared up, too stunned to move.

The raindrop hit the scaffolding, against all expectations, with a hollow bloing.

The bubble rebounded, sending the mezzanine swaying. Chicken felt like he had just been flattened by a squishy boulder.

For a brief moment, the bubble hung in the air as if thinking about what it should do next.

Then, having decided, the bubble burst.

A torrent of frigid, salty water hit the mezzanine and the pot, drenching Chicken and suffocating him. The ocean water sluiced into the stew and over the fire. A wave rolled over the audience, sending them to the ground. The sounds of rushing water, screams of terror, hissing fire, and splintering wood overtook Chicken's senses. The weight of the water hitting it again, the amateurish scaffolding gave away.

Chicken fell harshly to the ground.

He thought in bewilderment that he would drown in, of all places, a wasteland goblin encampment.

Then it was over.

Chicken coughed violently. The air filling his lungs was much more humid and salty than he was accustomed to. Sitting up, he saw the goblins were still completely floored. They lay around in various states of unconsciousness.

He also saw the beloved mushroom sitting innocently within arm's reach.

This was the moment of his daring escape. Who else but Chicken, mighty hero of legend, would have not only survived capture by cannibal goblins, but also would have taken their holy relic. The catalyst to their ritual slaughter.

So he took the mushroom and ran, the sounds of his plodding feet slapping the wet ground, while dazed and waterlogged goblins slowly got their bearings.

He took no notice of the pile of limp kelp laying motionless nearby.

**** "Stop! Stop him, he's getting away!"Stormhaegen had the screen analog in both hands, shouting at it like an invested sports fan. The mice clung to the edges, unperturbed. This is a metaphor for the ineffable, after all, and they were in no danger of being shaken off.One mouse tut-tutted."It was close, but that only matters with horseshoes, not holy men. Anyway, you're caught up now." Both mice detached from the screen. They scurried back to their transcription.The storm god pulled his attention from the clairvoyance device."What do horseshoes have to do with it?""It's a mortal saying," the other mouse said. But Stormhaegen didn't hear. He was already heading for the exit."I'm going out again," was all he said. "Getting a bit liberal with the miracles ," one of the mice said. The snide hook stopped Stormhaegen."And why shouldn't we be?" His hand was effectively on the door handle as he spoke, not looking at the mice. "There's more to life than paying bills, Scribb. At some point it's time to stop listing and start living." The sounds of writing stopped. "What have you done that's beautiful lately? It's a messy process, making beauty. Progress doesn't stay in lock step with quota."Scribb didn't answer, instead fostering a silence, which Stormhaegen broke after some moments."You should get out more. Take a walk. Loosen up, you know?" He smiled mischievously and added, "You might find the experience...mice." He left immediately.One of Scribb groaned, but despite himself, the other snickered.Outeb showed no reaction, impassively watching the clairvoyance machine follow the golden kobold as it fled with its prize.

Chapter 4 - Special Ingredient

Chicken was running. He liked running. This was because while Chicken was running, he wasn't being pummeled and bitten by the horde behind him. And so, Chicken liked running.

This wasn't just a flat-out foot race against the angry mob, however, because the terrain in the geyser field wasn't laid flat. It was broken, like a smashed ceramic plate amidst a pile of other smashed ceramic plates. The rocks jutted out of the ground, laying on top of one another at odd angles, baking in the noon day sun. The horizon flickered with illusory water. Chicken hastily clambered up a steep incline and leapt down to the surface below, his scales protecting his skin from the blistering rocks.

He grabbed a large and twiggy scrub bush, its roots clinging to a vertical surface for dear life, for a quick right turn. He bunny-hopped down each haphazard surface to the next incline. Try as it might, the jagged path was no major hindrance and he masterfully maintained his momentum and balance. Chicken climbed and slid and clambered all while carrying the large brown mushroom in the crook of his scaly arm. He juggled it constantly to free up either hand, elbow, shoulder, or to shift his weight to maintain his pace and course.

A calamity was chasing him, the mob hurling insults in Gobbledygook. They were incomprehensible, but stung him nonetheless. They were certainly words more heinous than "thief". The goblin language is increasingly versatile in that any phrase may be augmented to yield insult. Chicken had no way of knowing, but he was being described in acute detail, every aspect of him cursed and likened to all manner of slime, ichor, and unpleasantness. It was like an exacting verbal portrait, from a palate of raw sewage, on the expansive side of a hog.

Chicken looked back, despite his better judgement. He had yet to see the body of the calamity, the mob of goblins angry at him for stealing their precious mushroom. For interrupting and ruining their goblin boil. They had no reason to believe he wasn't the cause of the drop of water that had fallen from the sky, so they channeled their malice into the chase. The riotous tide of sharp-toothed, red-eyed, pallid-skinned, dirt-encrusted goblins from the goblin encampment scourged hand and foot over the obstacles with none of Chicken's grace, but with bonus points for passion. The nose slits on their faces flared with effort, keeping their bodies moving and curses flying. The long pointy ears on either side of each head bobbed in all directions with the constant motion.

Luckily for Chicken, the few with crude or rusty weapons were in the back of the mob, slower for being unable to use of both hands. But it was a mere consolation. The ones in front were liable to get the job done before a blade could ever reach his skin. He instantly regretted the glance. It might be the last thing he ever saw.

Up ahead, the terrain looked hopeful. A wall of red rock in the distance. It was debatably less dangerous than a mob of angry goblins. Chicken ducked under a desiccated log as he slid down a short incline, only to start climbing the sheer face of the cliff in front of him. He hoped it had enough hand holds to get him to the top of the seven foot rise. It was his only choice in this dead end, and the mob was gaining. Hand over hand with steadily deliberation, he ascended.

Halfway up, Chicken slipped and he lost purchase. His left side swung out. He clung tighter to his prize while painfully digging his claws into the stone. If it was hot from the sun, he couldn't tell and didn't care. The mushroom was making it hard for him to climb. He stole another glance at the enraged goblins, who were quickly approaching the base of the cliff, and decided he was close enough to the top for this next maneuver.

He chucked the giant mushroom over the ledge above him.

With his hands free, he could recover his grasp and make it to the top. A lucky throw saw the mushroom sail above the top of the wall and out of sight. Hopefully nothing carried it away by the time he got up. It was the only evidence of his tale, if he could make it out alive to tell it.

He started scrabbling up the last yard with both hands. A last heave at the top and he had made it, face down but over the ledge. With his snout against the hot dusty rock, he took a moment to catch his breath. His lungs hurt, his mouth was starting to dry out, and his muscles burned. Come to think of it, his joints ached slightly too. Judging by the sound, the calamity grew closer, congregating at the bottom.

So colorful was the goblin language, he couldn't hear any of the curses being used twice this whole time.

He pushed himself up on his knees and looked down at them. They weren't making great progress. Even as he watched, the highest lost their grip, falling heavily to the ground again. They hadn't even made it halfway.

One goblin wasn't even making an effort. It stood on a stone behind the rest and looked up at Chicken, frowning.

Chicken recognized it as the chef goblin.

It pointed a large wooden paddle up at him and spoke something garbled, mostly unheard among the rabble. Chicken shrugged and backed away from the ledge. A half-dozen stones sailed over and pelted him, and he recoiled. Rock chuckers.

Counterintuitively, he felt relief at the pelting of rocks. Goblins would fight a closed door before looking for a window. If they were struggling this hard, then he had time to grab the mushroom and finally lose them.

He scanned the area.

There was some greenery up here, and some puddles among the pitted landscape. Evidence of a nearby geyser. Despite having actively sought it out, the implications nonetheless opened a pit in his belly. Young kobolds, younger than Chicken, learned to fear and avoid the geysers near their home. The store of wild magic that ran under the land, mingling with the geothermal energy and subterranean mineral water, was powerful. There were unpredictable and potentially deadly effects ready to be wrought upon the unwary. In the geyser field, water meant wild magic, and wild magic meant danger. Almost as much danger as a mob of vengeful goblins.

He searched for the brown football-sized mushroom among the steps, swoops, branches, puddles, and alkaline colors. Everything looked a little organic, and not unlike the mushroom. How good was his throwing arm, really? The brown cap had a little heft to it, that is true, but it wasn't particularly aerodynamic. How bouncy was it? It looked fleshy, like it would plat instead of bloing, but maybe its looks we're deceiving.

The sooner I find it, Chicken thought, the sooner I get out of here. His thoughts wandered as he tried to weave this into the narrative for those at home. Chicken, goblin-bane. Chicken, geyser-walker. He weighed the two. Both had an impressive overtone, but he thought they didn't sound great together. Maybe if he used them in his story they would inspire an even better title. A noise pulled him out of his daydream and he looked back at the ledge.

A solitary goblin had just managed to clamber onto his level. Chicken was out of time. He would have to give up on his prize and return to the group empty-handed, with no proof of his escapades. They would scoff, or worse, they would laugh at the recount of his heroic deed. He couldn't give up yet. He batted bushes and kicked rocks. The goblin behind him, not stopping for a rest, rasped a shrill war cry.

There! In the shadow of a scraggly scrub lay the mushroom.

The goblin charged Chicken.

He dove, hurling himself against the prickly bush, the twigs snapping or vainly scraping against his sturdy scale armor.

The goblin was almost on top of him, and here he was, prone, with the mushroom on his belly like an otter with a clam.

In desperation, he opened his mouth fiercely and gave a reptilian hiss.

HHHHSSSSSSS!

It was somehow louder than even Chicken had expected, and something went ping in the goblin's head.

It froze.

The hiss, and Chicken's sharp teeth and claws, gave it pause. It realized for the first time that it was no longer in a mob. The goblin's face shifted from anger to concern at this epiphany, and it lowered its arms. They stared at each other.

Before the goblin could mentally change gears, it realized its legs were shaking. This was not because of fear but due to a sub-audible tectonic rumble.

The ground hissed again. A final warning.

The stone exploded in a torrent of hot water and pulsing auras.

Chicken covered his head, protecting his vitals from falling debris, scalding water, and the intense rainbow colors.

When all was clear, he looked again. There was no more goblin.

Looking around, he noticed some new goblins had just made it over the ledge to see the spectacle, their faces plastered with astonishment.

He counted his limbs and felt his face. Satisfied he was still whole, and apparently still Chicken, he composed himself. Fighting wobbly legs, he stood up while carefully maintaining eye contact with the closest goblin.

Hesitantly, coping with his sudden success, he said, "I'm keeping this. Don't take any more steps or you'll really get it. I'm serious."

He didn't know if any of the goblins spoke his language or not, but he felt he needed to say something. If they did understand, the things made no sign of comprehension. They just stood there, dumbly, with that same worried look. The same look he had seen on the goblin that was no more.

Backing slowly from the goblins before turning to run, Chicken stole away with the mushroom.

Chicken was running.

****

The mixture of half-steam, half-scalding water blasted through Kthakrk's soft, slimy body right as the thief-lizard had hissed at him. It had taken another couple of moments for the water to clear and for the thief-lizard to run away with the tribe's Secret Ingredient.

Despite this, Kthakrk didn't feel like chasing it.

He didn't feel like much at all.

"Well now, let's have a look at you," a voice said. It hadn't been Kthakrk.

It was a weary voice. A kindly voice.

When the former goblin turned to look at the speaker, Kthakrk discovered it had come from a short old lady in a plain dress and apron. Her curly brown hair came down just past her ears, framing an elegantly wrinkled face, which featured a pair of intelligent eyes. She was sitting on nothing.

She hovered solidly in the air, lounging on an unseen bar stool or similar. Next to her was a tray of cookies, similarly sitting on an unseen table.

The old woman, who was not goblin, nor human, nor anything but what Kthakrk could describe as "old woman", held between two fingers a short, thin white stick which Kthakrk didn't recognize. One end of the stick smoldered with a wisp of smoke curling up from it. She held it to her lips and breathed in through it, exciting the ember with the rush of air, and then breathed out a plume of smoke.

She stood laboriously and walked the few steps to the disembodied goblin.

He asked her a question in his own chaotic tongue.

"You are dead, Kthakrk," she replied, seeming to have understood. "The geyser blasted you quite thoroughly." Her tone of voice was threadbare and well-worn.

Kthakrk was shocked at how adeptly she pronounced his name. He was doubly so when he realized that he could understand her.

The goblin asked another question, the sound of someone gently smashing lightbulbs on wet sand with a rock.

She listened patiently, sympathetically.

"No, it wasn't that kobold's doing," she said with something like fossilized compassion. "It was just time for the geyser to blow. It's best not to dwell on it. Especially not you. Not now."

She added the last part hastily, before Kthakrk could hammer out a rebuttal from walnut shells and smashed bricks.

"There is something else you can do instead," she said, reaching over to the hovering tray. "Eat this cookie."

She held up a chocolate chip cookie the size of a saucer. Kthakrk had never seen a saucer, much less a cookie.

"Tell me all about your collection of shiny things. I know you keep it in that box you don't tell anyone about. I've been watching you with interest, and I can't say I've seen a more impressive store of trinkets than those you've been curating."

The genuine interest in her voice caused the goblin to grow excited. Kthakrk took the cookie.

Not pausing to chew between bites, Kthakrk gabbled to Death about his bits of shell and metal ores.

As he talked, she nodded and asked questions.

The two faded, and Kthakrk thought his last thought in this world.

He thought it a damn good cookie.

Chapter 5 - Tall Tales

"Pointing at the ground I told the filthy goblin, 'Not another step! Or I will be forced to use my magic on you. I will defend myself to the death.' But it was stupid and must have thought I was lying."

Chicken had arrived home, to the village in which he had been hatched and raised. It was the village they called Very Small Numbers. The name was largely due to a cross-lingual misunderstanding, the founders borrowing words from invaders.

The invaders had expressed difficulty in finding kobolds in "very small numbers", and the kobolds delivering their words, and so too the recipients of the message, took the concept as one of a kobold paradise and promised land. Whether or not the name indeed acted as a lucky charm, these kobolds had for many generations enjoyed the peace resulting from being undisturbed by aggressors.

Wasting no time, he had secreted his scavenged treasures in his safe spot. Later he would deliver his gift of ant eggs to his Auntie.

As he had meandered home, he had stopped to exploit nature's bounty. It was no hero's feast, but the hodge-podge of little treats had sustained him. The goopy innards of a succulent plant here, a brown slime-mold there.

He had even had the good fortune to find some ants while he was collecting tinder.

Digging his hand into the humid dirt, he had turned it over, revealing a chaotic mess of tiny chitinous bodies. Their tiny ant minds had been seized by insectile panic. Among the shiny black roiling mass, Chicken had located the white ant eggs, the larvae of the ants, some of which already in the process of being carried back into the dark.

Warriors had bravely defended the nest. They sprayed the invader with formic acid. The infantry charged, taking their menacing mandibles to the enemy.

The defense was to no avail.

None of it could penetrate Chicken's scales.

While he had scavenged, he had thought about the encounter with the goblins, replaying how he had been captured, how he had escaped, and how he had narrowly avoided being pummeled and left for dead in the wastelands.

He had played with the memories like they were clay, reimagining the base experiences, adding embellishments, like more goblins and longer fangs. All that was left was to show it to someone, and he had found a sufficient audience to practice telling his most recent tale.

Before him sat a half dozen children, the oldest at least a generation younger than him. They listened with varying degrees of amusement. Most had the air of having nothing better to do.

"At my command, the ground began to tremble! I could tell it scared because its evil sneer was gone. When suddenly," and here

Chicken jumped from his seat in a boisterous imitation, startling the younger kobolds.

With a shrug he said calmly, "It was gone."

One of the young kobolds, past the age of naiveté, scoffed. Chicken recalled his name was Brufon.

"You can't face down goblins." It was accusatory.

"I can too," Chicken rebutted. "I can and did."

"I don't believe it. Not for one minute."

Another one, Krepin, jumped in, saying "Yeah. You told Brother that you scared off a mutant coyote, but it was just a mangy runt."

His pride bruised, he fabricated wildly, "It was a mutant, and it only looked like a mangy runt after I was done with it. Anyway, how can I be lying if I have this?"

He produced the brown mushroom from behind his seat. He held it up proudly.

"It's just a mushroom, Chicken," Brufon said, perplexed.

Blustered, he defended himself. "No! No, it's the mushroom. The one from my story!"

One of the younger kobolds stood up to both of them. He remembered her from most of the other times he told his stories. She would always sit in front. She was named Pithy.

"Yeah! It is the mushroom! Chicken is brave!"

He nodded at this, thankful for her interceding on his behalf.

Before he could thank her, Brufon had snatched it away.

"Hey!" Chicken and Pithy shouted, but Brufon passed it to Krepin, holding the two kobolds back with an upraised finger.

"It's not the mushroom. It's just a mushroom," he said snidely.

"Eugghh!" Krepin interjected, "and it tastes awful." He had taken a surreptitious bite, and now was trying to get the taste off his tongue.

Brufon shrugged. "No use for it, then. Give it here." He held it out to Chicken, who grabbed at it, but pulled it away at the last second. He hucked it towards the edge of the camp.

"That's not nice, Brufon!" Pithy said tersely.

"Go get your garbage, Chicken!" he shouted. The two bullies laughed.

"Him? Taking on hundreds of goblins? I'll believe it when I see it," Krepin said as they walked away.

Pithy, his valiant defender, consoled him as the rest of the audience dispersed.

"I like your stories, Chicken."

He smiled at this as he looked out to where the mushroom had flown.

Suddenly Pithy remembered something.

"Oh! I almost forgot. Auntie wanted to see you when you got back. She told me specially to let you know. You need to bring stew."

"Me? Why?"

The little girl shrugged, and Chicken deliberated. Would he go retrieve the mushroom, or would he go seeAuntie right away? He weighed the encounter with untold angry goblins againstconfronting Auntie after a period of what she would call dilly-dallying.

Leaving his prize wherever it had landed for now, Chicken headed to the nearest bubbling pot.

****

Ducking to clear the low door of the bivouac, Chicken entered the dark and smoky tent where Auntie did her everyday magic.

By the low light of the smoldering oven, he could make out the shapes of her various stores of ingredients. Clusters of large clay pots and racks of stoppered bottles lined the walls, keeping the middle of the flat dirt floor mostly clear. Bundles of herbs hung from the ceiling by twine.

Chicken knew from memory not to fear anything Auntie left within reach. She usually kept the dangerous stuff hidden, or high off the ground, far from curious grabby claws that may wander into her tent.

Auntie was kneeling with her back to the door over something lumpy Chicken couldn't recognize in the dark.

He crept closer, wary of the situation. A little extra caution around Auntie was always warranted. She was mumbling to herself as she knelt in front of... A pile of blankets? A body?

He thought someone might have taken ill, but Pithy would have told him if it was sickness in the family.

He almost stumbled when Auntie abruptly called to him. She hadn't given any other sign she knew he was there.

"Give me the stew. I'll be busy with this one for a while."

An old scaled claw was extended from behind her cloak at him, not turning or looking up from what she was doing.

He placed the stone bowl in it and it was reeled back in.

"Fetch me the spoon from over there."

She indicated a small wooden spoon sitting on one of the jugs pulling overtime as a table across the room.

Chicken strafed over to it and picked it up, enraptured by the mysterious body over which Auntie had resumed mumbling.

As he came closer, spoon in hand, he saw the blanket was pulled up to the chin, but the head sticking out not that of a kobold.

No scales, just smooth skin. It had a pig like nose, and large tusks at the corners of the mouth forcing a scowl on the sleeping face.

It had black hair and, from where Chicken could see, it started into braids.

Auntie took the spoon, as Chicken was too distracted to hand it over.

"We found this orc dehydrated and unconscious less than a mile from here the other day. Judging from the wounds and age, I say we've recovered an exile."

She lifted its head and spooned some broth between the orc's lips.

Chicken whispered, "Why are we helping him?"

Auntie looked at him for the first time, a sudden and hard look like flint on iron.

She said firmly, "We're helping her because we found her. She's our responsibility until she's better and can fend for herself."

Auntie's features softened when she realized she had startled him.

"I'm sorry Chicken. I see now it was an innocent question. Salander-"

She almost added something else, but instead turned back and dribbled another spoonful.

As Chicken watched, he could see the orc's consciousness move under the surface of her sleep. She stirred and spoke gruffly but quietly. Auntie relayed the translation.

"She has been saying she's not an orc. If I had to guess, she has lost who she is, and it disquiets her spirit. There are more wounds to tend once her body has healed."

Auntie started singing a song as she fed the sleeping orc.

It was one known well by Chicken and his cousins, since Auntie had sung it to them when they were hatchlings.

The tune was a soft lullaby and told a story about the fabled Desert Hare and how he tricked the evil queen of the desert, driving her away and bringing rain to his people.

It was Chicken's favorite story, and it had become a kind of lens through which he viewed his own experiences.

Chicken identified with clever Desert Hare, who was always portrayed in his stories as brave, resourceful, and generally well-liked, but the song always sounded sad, despite the heroic victory over evil.

Auntie had told him of their tribe's kinship with the queen, that every kobold she reared could trace their lineage back to her.

Being too young for independent thought, Chicken had grown around that grain of knowledge, taking it as indisputable fact.

Auntie finished the stew around the verse where Hare rallied Ant and his cousins to march on the queen. She put the bowl down and stopped singing.

The orc had not rejected the food, but was still submerged beneath the placid surface of unconsciousness.

Auntie gestured for Chicken to come around and help her to her feet. She picked up her cane and, with all three supports beneath her, the two of them left the tent.

Chapter 6 - Love and War

A merigo coughed and spluttered as his lungs filled with air for the first time in years. This sudden and painful experience was one of a hundred he was currently dealing with.

The bubble of seawater had absorbed most of the impact from his crash from cruising altitude. The rest went into him.

He ran through the last few moments in his head in the slow-motion of traumatic memories.

The bubble fell fast and hard onto some kind of wooden structure, missing the bubbling pot, but hitting some kind of gnomeoid creature that was staring straight at him, dumbfounded. The bubble rebounded before giving way and subjecting him to the full and unmitigated force of gravity. He, amidst a torrent of water, hit the landing. The whole platform gave away.

Everything was still wet.

Wetness, too, was a feeling he would also have to learn to deal with. Underwater, one never feels wet. It is only when one is dragged on land, out in the open air on dry land, could one feel the water on their skin.

Right now, he wished to be far below the surface with his fish and corals. That thought carried a snag to it, but he couldn't place...

Fen!

He pulled his hat off and retrieved the pipe. The crustacean wouldn't come out, though it still clung to his uprooted hairs. He put the pipe to his lips and blew. The crab popped up like a salty party popper, startled but fine.

Just checking.

Fen grumpily retreated again, and Amerigo returned him to his cap.

For the first time, he noticed the bodies strewn about the place, moaning and writhing. A shout grabbed his attention. One of the creatures, wearing a very wet and droopy hat, was going about the place kicking the others. He was spurring them to action.

Amerigo didn't like his tone of voice. It didn't give him much hope for an amicable seeing-off.

He decided it best to become scarce while a war party got to its feet around him. He left the encampment by the way opposite the crowd was moving before anyone had the wits to call him out.

****

Hours later, Amerigo was still walking.

The effort wasn't what bothered him. He wasn't buff, but swimming underwater as he did was great exercise. What bothered him was the hot sun and dry air. Something of his god's protection was still about him. He was coated in a thin salty membrane. Or maybe it was just sweat. He was incredibly thirsty for the first time in years, too.

He didn't bother removing his cap. It blocked some of the sun while also providing Fen with a much-needed humid microclimate. The crab was a hearty breed, capable of great feats of land exploration by special means of keeping his gills wet. He just wasn't very useful.

The gnome had encountered some wildlife along the way. A lizard had been sunning itself on a rock when it was rudely interrupted by Amerigo. It had stared at him blankly while he expressed friendship and inquiry. The lizard responded with a slow blink. It scurried out of sight leaving Amerigo feeling like he'd been misunderstood. This had never happened to him before.

The bird was a success, however. A big black one with a pink bald head had been following him for some time. He took it as a good omen. Plus-one new friend, even if it was a little standoffish.

What really bothered Amerigo, aside from the strength-sapping oppressive sun persistently hovering over his shoulder like a bad office supervisor, were the rocks. It wasn't that there were so many, though it was drudgery itself to make his way among them compared to the freedom of swimming.

The rocks weren't alive.

Coral was a unique marriage of stone, animal, and plant, and he dreadfully missed being among it. Its inhabitants could be called denizens, and the lush formation a neighborhood. In this horrible place was only fungus and selfish hissing critters. There was the occasional bloom of sticks that was either dead scrub, or something merely so dormant in its patient wait for the rare flood waters as to be temporarily dead scrub.

These arid rocks were an oppressed inner city by comparison.

Ultimately, he was lost in a foreign country without a phrase-book. He was tired from sleeplessness, fatigued by the terrain, and very close to heatstroke. He collapsed on the ground.

It was the perfect time for a religious moment.

"Amerigo!"

He was too tired to look around. The voice called again. He thought he recognized it through the mind fog. It was like it was booming from far off, like a thunderstorm on the horizon.

"Get up! I can't believe you could miss him like that!"

It wasn't angry at him. It was jovial, in fact. It chided him in a friendly manner, a verbal shoulder punch. Amerigo could feel the warm rock under him, but was steadily caring less and less.

"That kobold is the one you're looking for, Amerigo."

Kobold? What is a kobold?, he thought, close to sleep.

"Don't move. I can restore you a bit, and I'll rustle up some help."

At those words, a shadow crept over him. A blessed cumulus cloud had spontaneously appeared, blocking the sun. To the delight of both him and a nearby dead scrub, it began to rain.

****

Justafar and Eleruse were taking wine in their orcish longhouse while watching the servants fight to the death. It was an enjoyable pastime the two preferred in each other's company, though Justafar was not in his usual bloodthirsty mood. Eleruse was taking notice and chided him with a bark.

"If you aren't enjoying the fight, I'm calling it off to save on servants."

He only grumbled and muttered into his wine, so she signaled irritably to the servants to stop. The goblin and lizardfolk froze in a picture of chaos.

The lizardfolk stood hunched over the goblin, with the goblin wringing the lizard's neck and the lizardfolk in the middle of yet another punch to the goblin's midsection. The two quickly separated and groveled backwards out of the room.

Neither of the orcs noticed. Eleruse was lovingly glaring daggers at Justafar, while he sulked in his wine, simultaneously thinking politics and recognizing his woman's concern. She stood from her throne and pointed at him.

"Stop your sulking or you'll feel my hand, worm," she growled.

This show of affection snapped him fully out of his reverie and he responded to her in kind.

"Shut up! I'll sulk as much as I like, cur."

She could tell his heart wasn't in it. She spat on the ground at his feet and taunted him.

"What's wrong?" she asked with a sneer.

"I've been thinking about Lord Kairon. His orders lately haven't been any different. More of the same. I don't agree with his policies."

Eleruse stood attentively facing her man, only thrusting her empty cup in her outstretched hand to the wine attendant standing blithely behind their thrones.

Justafar continued, "I understand that he's undefeated. I watched the whole fight between him and Chief Ironskull, the whole three days it lasted. It's just..." he trailed off meekly. She reacted to the sudden passivity of his words, so he ended it instead by beating his fist on the arm of his throne and roaring, to show he wasn't upset at her.

"Idiot. How could this be upsetting you? He is undefeated. His right to lead is apparent."

"He may have the right, but I question his morals. Do you not remember Kithbar demanding to see Lord Kairon's skull collection? What kind of leader hides the collected skulls of his enemies?"

"You complete fool. Lord Kairon himself said it was beyond counting."

"Where are they, then?," the halls shook with the force of his words. "We should see the mountain from here, if his words are true. Lately I'm wondering if he still knows how to use a sword correctly with what he's been telling us to do with them."

"You're talking about his plan to subjugate the very earth into feeding our people. I say we should have thought of it sooner."

At this he cut her off. "He's commanding us to beat them so that we may carve the earth with them!" He was shocked anew at the ridiculous notion. "The ground don't bleed! It...it's unnatural!" With that, he slumped in his chair.

He had a point. Lord Kairon's kind of leadership was like none the orcs had seen before. She could only manage a half-hearted, "Idiot." A brief pause framed the moment before she strode over and slapped him.

"Arrange a party," she commanded, "Go out and conquer. I don't want you in here getting soppy."

He was comforted that she agreed with him, and glad to have vented his frustration. His thoughts turned intimate at the slap. He stood abruptly, the two standing chest to chest, faces locked in matching grimaces. Without looking, he waved the wine servant out of the room, who nervously complied just as the fight started. Justafar felt lucky to have such a loving partner. His head locked in her elbow and his back bent double, he thought about how he loved her to death.

****

Justafar and his hunting party were on the prowl. Armed with the few weapons untouched by Kairon's mandate, they tramped about the wastelands looking for objects of their wrath and savages to imprison. It had been a while since they'd had some old fashioned orcish fun. They had celebrated the occasion with drink when they were first out of sight of the village walls.

Village? No, Kairon had another word for it. He wanted everyone to call it a city.

Out here were the so-called farmlands. Their great leader had the ridiculous notion that if they attacked the earth and desecrated its wounds with the corpses of vegetables, they would profit in some esoteric way. Some orcs had been assigned to the duty, criminals allowed to work off their debt to society. While his party was sitting and drinking, he could see one of the poor devils toiling away.

After drinking half their ration of orcish ale, the party wandered drunkenly through the wilderness. Orcs are particularly hardy, being typically tall, musclebound, and having some resistance to the elements. They had little to fear from exposure. Those elements which would normally eat a sleeping kobold in two snaps would have to think twice before imposing themselves on a wayward orc.

Justafar was only loosely acting on information about a goblin camp near the vill-…city. Goblins didn't make the best laborers, but small gangs made good sport and were not very hard to find. There were always plenty to fill the prisons.

In his own opinion, lizardfolk made the best laborers. They were individualistic, strong, and without much in the brain department. He couldn't tell if they even knew they were imprisoned because, to him, their lives only improved when they came under the protection of the orcs. Food was more plentiful, and they only occasionally had to fight for their life, compared to the everyday occurrence it was in the wild. It seemed that way to Justafar, anyway, not that he thought of it often or in depth.

It was while they were looking for this goblin camp that one of the orcs reported something strange.

"A single cloud, sire, over there and not too far off." The orc was pointing at it as he spoke. "It's not the rainy season, and it's all by itself. Something important over there."

Justafar grunted a confirmation. He selected two of his group and they set off eagerly.

****

The water cooled the rock and drenched Amerigo's kelpy clothing. He started to come around. Had the voice said it was going for help? He opened his eyes and looked around, now fully sensible.

"Look what it is," a voice said, much more gruff and less jovial than he had expected, "some sort of...soggy goblin by the looks of it."

Chapter 7 - Hurraggh

Amerigo had been travelling with the orcs who captured him. It was the first time they stopped since taking him into their custody, and the orcs were removing their packs and resting.

"Hey," someone said.

He caught what was tossed to him. An impressive fluke given his hands were bound.

"Eat," the orc told him.

It was a hunk of dried and salted meat. Amerigo reluctantly chewed it, barely a mouthful in all. Something blocked the sun, causing him up look up.

"Water," this orc said. He was carrying an oversized water skin, ready to pour it over the gnome. They didn't trust him not to drink more than his ration. It was humiliating, but Amerigo opened his mouth. The water hit him full in the face.

The orc laughed and walked away, leaving Amerigo wiping himself off. It wasn't wholly uncomfortable. The water was cool, and he drank some of what he wiped off. His hat was moist now, which was a bonus for Fen. There was no telling what the orcs would do if they learned of his friend, so the crab would remain a secret. Amerigo returned to chewing his meal.

He thought about when they had found him.

"Read it the thing," one of the two orcs had said.

"What thing?"

"The thing we read to the prisoners now, idiot. They're not our prisoners if we don't read 'em the thing. Makes it official, Lord Kairon says."

"Oh, right. The thing."

At that, the orc drew a scroll and read from it.

"Savage wasteland creature:

You is, er... captured by the city of Hurraggh. Do not, uh, try n' get out. You is a prisoner, charged of the crime of not being an orc... an' for bein' slower'n us. Anythin' you say can an' will be used against you on the grounds of shuttin' you up.

Welcome to our great orc nation."

After the puzzling ritual, Amerigo wondered if that was what had really been on the scroll, and how much had been improvised.

Mere moments after he swallowed his food, the group was up and moving once more.

It was only a few days into his bondage and he was getting pretty good at doing things with his wrists touching. The boulders were everywhere throughout the desert. Rocks that came up to an orc's waist were looming obelisks. But he dared not fall behind. These musclebound giants meant business, knew the terrain, and had the only water. He did his best to keep up.

He wasn't abused by the orcs. Aside from giving him incentive to follow orders, they ignored him. Amerigo wondered how long this state of affairs would continue. It would be best to start scheming for ways out, though he'd prefer not to be lost in the desert again.

The nights were cool and dark. The orcs had no need to light camp fires. One or two looked a bit more miserable for the lack of light and heat. Amerigo mused on this, thinking it would attract unwanted attention, but he wouldn't have imagined it was because they didn't want to appear vulnerable to one another.

They ate little from their packs, mostly dried meat, and rarely spoke. The little language they used was almost purely informational, devoid of emotion. No threats at each other, though no thanks either. They were bereft of banter and song. It made Amerigo feel colder.

As far as he could tell, the troop of orcs was wandering aimlessly in the wastes. It was all bland, featureless rock to him. He could only hope they weren't going in circles. Along the way they had contributed further to their capture of wasteland savages.

They had come across a pair of lizardfolk, who were shackled, informed of their imprisonment, and bidden to fall in line. They didn't put up much of a fight, which was a bit odd to Amerigo because they seemed generally healthy and of a good disposition. Despite this, they looked almost willing to be taken into custody.

Amerigo found them to be particularly friendly toward him. He supposed there was some intrinsic link, or common denominator, between lizardfolk and the denizens of his reef. Perhaps their intelligence filled the gaps in his druidic phrasebook. At any rate, they weren't snippy or indifferent to him.

On another occasion, the orcs captured most of a group of goblins. The whole affair looked something like a few adults playing a game of tag with a playground of toddlers, except much rougher. The goblins bit and scratched when the orcs picked them up, apparently forgetting the weapons they carried. Most of them dropped their makeshift pikes and spears when they were picked up.

Only one was putting forth a concerted effort into rebellion. It was a goblin wearing a chef's hat and swinging a wooden paddle. It held off two orcs, who weren't keen on getting a smart crack, until a third flanked him.

The rest of the group fully dispersed after each orc caught about four goblins. Amerigo was certain they would have to let some go for lack of restraints, but they conjured hobbles, shackles, chains, locks, and even a portable stockade. Somehow or another, all the goblins were detained.

That night, Amerigo couldn't get any sleep for the constant chittering of gobbledygook. The one which had the paddle earlier had been the ring-leader for an escape attempt. Being made by goblins, which is to say "badly", they had woken their captors with the incessant banging of rocks on locks. The orcs resolved this by gagging the leader. Without his provocative chittering, the rest decided to call it quits and everyone was able to sleep more peacefully.

A night after that, Amerigo had woken from much needed rest to one of the lizardfolk making anxious noises and trying to pull away from its restraint. It didn't respond at all to Amerigo trying to calm it.

Weakened by the cold night, it was putting all of its energy into getting away, pulling at its tether. Amerigo could see only panic in its eyes. Something was driving it wild with fear.

He turned to follow its gaze. It was looking at the other lizard-folk, restrained at the other side of the camp. This one wasn't able to panic because there was a big cat sitting on it.

****

Hsshhshasasha couldn't breathe. It trembled under the massive dark paws pinning it to the cold ground. It could only watch as very slowly, very silently, the jaws came down to its throat, bit down, and pulled away with almost no resistance.

Moments later, Hsshhshasasha got up, leaving what was left of its body behind. This pure self-ness, possibly its soul, passed through the big cat eating the mortal remains. It did a quick self-check before scrambling away. There were two of it, one here, doing the looking, and one... all over the place. The camp was dark, but the lizardfolk could see other big cats converging on the sleeping orcs and goblins.

There was a blood curdling screech. Someone else had noticed the encroaching doom.

Suddenly, the camp was up in arms, except for those arms which were shackled. No one seemed to notice the lizardfolk who had died.

"We're in for a treat, Hsshhshasasha," a voice said.

It came from an old woman who was sitting on nothing next to the lizardfolk. There were several things odd about this, and they registered in the lizardfolk's mind in this order.

First, it recognized its name. She had pronounced it perfectly.

Secondly, when the lizardfolk looked at her, it didn't necessarily see an old human woman, or an old lizardfolk for that matter. Its brain filled in the details without really hitting the part of the brain that was Hsshhshasasha. It just saw what it interpreted as an old woman with short brown curly hair and wearing a plain dress and apron.

The final thing that the lizardfolk processed was the fact that this woman was clearly sitting, one leg over the other, on nothing. She was holding a cigarette in one hand and her elbow in the other. Hsshhshasasha knew what cigarettes were. It had often found them in the boxes of the trading wagons it had raided. Bitter things to eat, but the taste often lingered.

"More and more orcs lately have been dying of old age," she continued. "A sad state of affairs. They're always so disappointed."

She wasn't looking at Hsshhshasasha, but at the mounting defense of the orc camp. Each orc was fighting two cats at once. The atmosphere was full of blood and thunder. Axes were flying like yo-yos, knuckles were crunching bone, claws and teeth were rending flesh on both sides of the engagement. Hsshhshasasha, however, was not looking at the fight, but had crouched to investigate what the old woman was sitting on. It waved his hand under her. Nothing but air.

"You're the only casualty in this one. I haven't come for any others tonight." She took a drag on her cigarette, her gaze coolly fixed on the action. The orcs were frolicking. They poured into the night sky hoots and howls and war cries. It was the music of their souls.

Death put out her cigarette on nothing next to her and picked up a cookie the size of a saucer from beside the invisible ash tray.

"Things will be made right in the end," she said with a sigh, "and they'll start dying happier. I had to give up Ashley, but it's for the greater good. She has a valuable lesson to teach."

Hsshhshasasha couldn't find any supports at all holding her up. It had crawled under her completely by now.

"Hsshhshasasha," she said, standing and turning to him, "You are dead, if you haven't guessed." She handed him the cookie not unkindly.

It maneuvered into sitting cross-legged while it changed mental gears.

Dead?

It hissed sadly.

"Take the cookie. You'll feel better."

It clutched the cookie to its chest. It stared at a point on the ground in front of it and hissed like the slow release valve on an air compressor.

"You've got all the time in the underworld. If you need me, I'm here to talk."

And at this, the two faded.

****

The last of the cats was being slaughtered. The remains were being gleefully pummeled by the overzealous orcs, and the surrounding area was painted with viscera. By sunrise, the cats could have been juiced from the rocks.

The rest of the journey happened quickly to Amerigo. The encounter had put the orcs in a jaunty mood. This unfortunately meant a faster forced march and fewer breaks. They also jeered more at their captives now, too, which he thought was a nice touch. He and the rest of the alleged maggots not fit to squirm under the same sky as their shouting warden were eventually driven to the orc city of Hurraggh.

In the surrounding farmland, Amerigo saw orcs in straw hats moving rocks, shattering boulders, and hitting the softer parts of the ground with bent swords. There were thatch roof huts punctuating the farm plots. Houses or storage sheds, Amerigo mused.

Not long after, they had arrived at the gates of Hurraggh.

The walls to the city were stone, and very high. The portal was shuttered with large stone doors.

"Who that be?" came a shout from atop the wall.

"It's us. Open the gate, you blind slug."

There was a barely audible grumble from the orc on the gate, followed by the blast of a horn.

It went on for an orcish lungful, causing birds to scatter. It filled the air with a rich tone which bounced off the landscape and charged savagely into the sky. When it was over, the horn was placed back down and nothing else happened.

The orcs on the ground stared at the orc on the gate, who looked at the orcs on the ground. After a moment, the orc on the gate turned around.

"That means haul on the doors you idiots! Do I have to tell you every time? Get those whips moving, you good-for-nothing drivers! Now!"

The words were like magic. The massive stone doors started opening inward, leaving Amerigo awestruck. He marveled at the feat of engineering while the sound of stone scraping on stone rumbled around him. A shove to the back was required to get him moving with the rest of the troop.

Inside the walls, he saw more stone buildings, more thatch roof, more terracotta. He also saw more orcs, goblins, and lizardfolk. They milled about with purpose. Each orc was followed by a couple of lizardfolk or a handful of goblins. These were invariably carrying a pot or a sack, if not something heavier. Orcs were obviously accustomed to putting their prisoners to work.

Amerigo imagined a future of hauling heavy things, never seeing the reef again. The thought sunk into the pit in his belly.

While they were being marched up the street, a young orc came running at them, calling for Justafar. "Lord Kairon wants to see you. He sent me special to get you when you returned." He waved a piece of vellum.

Justafar snatched it and scowled at it. He turned to the troop as the young orc rushed off.

"Take these to the prisons for processing," he said, gesturing to the group of them. "Except this one."

At this, he grasped Amerigo by the shoulder, causing the gnome to gulp.

****

"We have picked over seven oases in their entirety, and still it is not enough."

Lord Kairon was in the building he referred to as Town Hall. He was thinking, as he always did, about Hurraggh. The topic of his musings at the moment was the city's consumption of plants. Orcs did require a certain amount of vegetation in their diets, it was true, but evidence of different kinds of consumption lay just outside the window.

A sector of the city lay sprawled before him. Blocky adobe buildings covered in thatch, the ends of wood struts poking through at the edges of walls and marking the occasional upper floor, comprised the layout. None of the ambitious two-story buildings reached nearly as high as his third-story offices.

"We cannot subsist on gathering to meet Hurraggh's needs," he continued.

The sounds of eating suffused the room, its point of origin being the long table to which Kairon had his back. Several orcs, decorated each in his own way, were picking at the food that consisted of the latest meal. Remnants of food littered the area around each of them even as they piled more in front of themselves. At the head of the table was an empty chair as dark and foreboding as it was lavish and prominent. Placed before it was a single plate, scoured of all traces of eating.

Kairon prepared himself while his cabinet was slowly sated. There was much to do, and foremost of his tools were the tribe chiefs. He had to convince them of their own need before he could sell them a solution.

"We need to adopt farming, and take hold of it with both hands."

There were roasted beasts of all manner, now mostly bones, the meat having been liberally seasoned and sauced. Small bowls of fruits and vegetables had been picked over, leaving the pits and seeds alongside any overripe or measly specimens behind. Attendants with jugs of water and wine were present to fill waiting goblets.

Kairon turned away from the window and strode back to his seat. Instead of sitting, he bent over and put both hands on the table, fixing each of the others with a look. An attendant moved to fill is cup, but he covered it with a hand. The attendant withdrew.

"Progress needs resources, and the land does not provide in the quantities we need." The plates of his ever-present dark armor clinked gently as he moved.

One of the diners waved a greasy hand deferentially and said, "Marrowcrack is ready to provide, my Lord. Already we have dedicated a dozen and a half prisoners and disseminated your, erm, tutorials." He ended the statement by biting into the roasted thigh he was holding, and had been studying while he spoke.

He continued with his mouth full, "But we must keep a modest number for the ceremonial prisoner arena coming up. Will anyone else contribute, or do we have to take this burden on ourselves? I challenge Boldbreak to contribute even half that number. How many have they given you, Lord?"

The accused slammed both hands on the table, almost tipping their drink.

"And where did you get the prisoners? Boldbreak makes up the majority of Kairon's police force, if you'll recall from discussions last season! We can't reduce our numbers and expect to maintain a street presence and a patrol outside the city!"

Marrowcrack floundered at this, the ball back in his court. He settled on a different target.

"I don't see any Skullcrush present. And why would that be? What contributions are they making to the progress of Hurraggh? I would have expected them to start sacrificing for the greater good by now. How long has it been since they joined our great orc nation, again? It didn't even take the Bloodboils this long."

But he had stepped on another foot. The Bloodboil chieftain's face grew stony and sullen. He growled, "Are you saying we ain't pulling our share, Marrowcrack?"

The name oozed and popped like cooling magma as it came out.

Kairon sighed and straightened up as yet another committee meeting devolved into insults and tusk-measuring. It was a behavior for which he never felt he fit, having no tusks of his own. All of his teeth stayed demurely in his mouth, unlike those of his kindred. If it weren't for his win-streak, they might use it against him. That, and the color of his skin, which was a sooty black, the same color as his armor, instead of the healthy green of an adult orc.

An attendant was at his elbow, and he allowed himself to be pulled aside. He endured a salute.

"Chief Justafar has arrived as you have commanded, my Lord."

"Please don't do that," Kairon sighed.

The attendant's face looked confused while his body remained at attention. "What should I not do, my Lord?"

"I've told you all time and again. Please don't salute me."

"Why wouldn't I salute you, my Lord?"

"Because you are an attendant, not a member of the military. Please send in Chief Justafar."

The attendant latched onto the order at the end, which was the only thing he understood. He saluted again and said, "Yes my Lord. As you command," and then sent a prisoner to send the message.

Kairon sighed again and returned to watch the proceedings. He dodged a flying bowl.

Justafar and Amerigo entered the room, unnoticed by the rest of the cabinet. Kairon slipped away and greeted the chief warmly. "Chief Justafar, welcome back. How was your hunting party?"

Justafar pocketed his disgust at his Lord's reception and prepared a response. He needed something that Lord Kairon wouldn't disapprove of, and which wouldn't make him hate himself.

"We slaughtered many beasts of the land and captured many of the indigenous creatures. It was," he paused, "a good hunt. My Lord."

"That's wonderful. I'm glad to hear it was successful. I do hope you and your troop enjoyed your time. Would you like some food? Some of it remains unsodden."

The other chiefs had liberally coated the immediate area around the table in scraps, but it was true that some was still edible. For now. Justafar decided to take this as an order and grunted, "Yes my Lord." This was the worst kind of torture. The kind that didn't touch the body, but went right through to the inside. Kairon was truly a terrible master.

He clapped his hands, each time his gauntlets ringing a soft clank, and spoke over the quibbling chiefs. Justafar picked at what remained of the meal.

"Everyone, Justafar has arrived. We will table the issue of acquiring bodies for farming for now, as we have other matters at hand. Justafar, I wish to discuss some minor matters in the merger of your tribe with the City of Hurraggh. It seems some of the old Boldbreak habits die hard, so a few of your tribesmen are currently recovering." The Boldbreak chief sat up straight, putting down the bare rib he was wielding to fix Justafar with a stern glare. "A couple of them attacked some innocent citizens in the streets, formerly of the Marrowcrack and Sharpteeth tribes." He tut-tutted. "One of them will make it, but the other, I'm afraid, succumbed to the loss of his lower half."

"We want reparations!" Marrowcrack shouted. "This was no honorable death!"

Justafar tried not to bridle at the outburst. He managed not to react vainly. "They sound like honorable warriors, to me. What would you have me do, my Lord?"

"We don't do that kind of thing any more, Chief Justafar," Kairon said before Marrowcrack could get a word in. "Please, in your own time, discourage this kind of behavior in the future. I'm sure the city would be most appreciative."

"Yes my Lord," Justafar said duly. "Would you have me flog them?"

"If you must. Eventually we will need harsher punishment for this kind of infraction in the future, but that will settle the matter for now."

Marrowcrack simmered, but was appeased.

Sharptooth said idly, "We do not begrudge you your victory." She grinned, displaying her namesake, the sharpened teeth her tribe cultivated. "We took...trophies."

Justafar's blood boiled at the thought of honest warriors being punished for slaughtering ancient enemies. If Kairon had not already bested him for supremacy over the tribe, he would challenge him in a heartbeat. As it stood now, however, it would be nothing but further dishonor. Justafar thought he should be dead, and it was dishonorable enough that he should go on living as a Chief under a Lord. He looked at the other chiefs through the now all-too-common haze of loathing that colored his interactions with Kairon. They all seemed content being Kairon's gaggle of second-fiddles.

The issue was, however, that Kairon couldn't be beaten by anyone in this room. It wasn't that Justafar and the others hadn't lost. They each would have been killed if that were the case, as the time-honored rules stood among the orc tribes. No, it was just that Kairon didn't lose. There was no punishment that he couldn't endure. There was no weapon that could pierce his skin and, so far, no orc who could best him.

He looked at his Lord again. Not a proper dark lord at all, but a sheep in wolf's clothing. The gentle calmness behind the reputation of terror and conquest. The farmer all warriors fear.

"That was all, Chief Justafar," he said, dismissing him politely.

"My Lord, I do have news from the hunt."

"News? What news?"

For the first time, he noticed Amerigo.

Chapter 8 - Teatime

C hicken entered Auntie's tent carrying a heavy earthen jar.

"Where do you want this fermented root, Auntie?" he asked, straining against the thing which was about the size of his torso. She had sent him to dig it up, noting this one was ready for the next stage of the process for the sanitization liquid it was used for. A clear, strong beer sloshed about in the sealed container.

Auntie didn't tell him, merely pointing to a collection of pots of similar make and size.

"Put it at the back, please, Chicken. I don't want to disrupt the order in which these have arrived."

There were at least a dozen of the jars arranged like bowling pins. He would have to move several out of the way to place this new one. Chicken sighed, or rather would have if the weight of the jar hadn't compressed it into a grunt on its way out. He set to the task.

Chicken liked helping his Auntie, if only for the sense of pride that came with her comments about the shortage of any real help nowadays.

As he crossed the room, he skirted the sleeping orc delicately. She had been here, sleeping, the whole of the three days since he had returned to Very Small Numbers from his excursion and the ordeal with the goblins and the mushroom. She still had that forced scowl on her face due to her tusks that so unnerved him. He had never encountered an orc himself, but he knew them to be an aggressive, short-tempered, direct kind of folk who put others at risk of doing work they didn't particularly like or elect to do. In the brief glance he took at her as he passed, he imagined her eyes opening suddenly. Horrible gimlets struggling to support an angry, furrowed brow.

That wasn't his imagination. Her eyes really did open. He felt pinned beneath the glare of the formerly sleeping orc, the first of however many living nightmares the stories had led him to imagine. Startled, he convulsed, flinging with sudden super-kolboldian strength the heavy earthen jar above his head. He yipped, but only heard it the instant it came back to him from across the room.

Auntie turned from her macrame to catch most of the action, involuntarily calling to Chicken to stop him from tossing the jar, which had already been tossed. It hung in the air in a perfect moment, directly above Chicken. The orc was no longer looking at Chicken, but the pot above him. The shift of its gaze dragged with it Chicken's attention. He too was now looking up at the heavy pot hanging precariously over him in this single prolonged moment, the one before which Chicken would be squashed like a bug beneath the massive ballistic jug of primitive alcohol.

Chicken felt the impact.

It didn't come from up above, but rather from below. And the thing that hit him didn't shatter and splash like one would expect a clay pot of fermented root juice, but rather wrapped around him and sent him sprawling backwards.

The pot shattered on the hard dirt floor of Auntie's hut.

Chicken looked up into the face of an orc. It was contorted into a look of concern.

"It takes three months for a batch to ferment properly," came Auntie's voice sullenly. "Not to mention how long it takes to make the pot."

The orc rolled off of Chicken and got to her feet, at first hitting her head against the relatively short roof, before standing awkwardly in a half bow.

"Get up, Chicken," Auntie said. "We need to prepare some tea for our guest. There is a pouch sewn into the wall over there in that shadow. Bring me a fistful of what's inside." She looked up at the menacing figure standing like an adult in a playhouse. "And you, have some sense and sit down. I don't need a skylight in here."

Miraculously, her words had immediate effect. The orc sat cross-legged where she had stood. Chicken was still only leaning on his elbows, half sitting up. Auntie rounded on him with the voice that commanded the orc.

"I said get up and get the tea, child. Now go."

With a glance at the silent orc, he did as he was told. Was she seething? Her breaths were deep and rapid, but she made no other sign about her emotional state.

Chicken retrieved the dried tea, which he recognized by smell as Auntie's stash of the good stuff, a blend of rare aromatics, dried. He also picked up a container of filtered water nearby and set it on the embers burning in Auntie's fire pit. Before long, it would start boiling, and the brew would be ready to serve. He set out three small cups and distributed the tea among them.

In that time, Auntie had stored her macrame and arranged a cushion with herself on top, facing the seated orc. It looked at the shattered pot and said, "I could clean it up. It wasn't my intention to startle that one."

Auntie waved a hand. To Chicken she said, "Get the blanket I've got rolled up, and the broom from by the door."

Chicken went to work sweeping the larger shards off to the side. When that was done, he put a rug down over the larger part of the spreading alcohol. When the tea began boiling, he prepared three cups. After serving the first to Auntie, he approached the orc hesitantly, glancing to the matriarch for security. She nodded, and he held out the cup.

The orc took it gently in both hands. "Thank you," she murmured.

Chicken picked up his own cup and sat next to the two of them, forming a kind of three pointed circle. Silence reigned as Chicken waited for either Auntie or this guest to talk. The scowl returned to the orc's face now as she stared down into her tea. He wondered if she didn't like it. He hadn't seen her take a sip, but his back had been turned as he got his own cup.

Blowing on his own tea, he started to drink. The flowery and earthy flavor drowned out the mineral sting of the spilled alcohol that filled the room. He finished, finding the orc glaring at him again, but she looked away.

"Is it soup?" she asked with a face like a battleaxe.

He proffered the cup, saying, "Tea." He took another drink to demonstrate.

"It is not salty like a broth or stock. Where does it come from?"

"I don't know. Auntie makes it."

"But she just ordered you to make it."

"All I did was finish it. She takes the dried flowers and bark and roots and stuff and mixes them up."

"You drink stewed plants." She said it flatly, her tone not reflecting the accusation in her expression.

Chicken didn't know how to sort this comment, letting it go without a response. Who doesn't drink tea?

"The plants are still in the water," the orc added.

"Leave them in there." This was Auntie speaking up for the first time. "I can read your fortune from the patterns when you're finished."

The orc looked at her briefly, then back at the cup. She swirled it slowly, watching the slow moving flecks.

"But I have the cup. I can control the pattern," she countered.

Auntie smiled mysteriously. "Perhaps. But then perhaps fate intervenes. Do you know how to shape the leaves to get what you want?"

Unbeknownst to Chicken and the rest of Very Small Numbers, the fortunes depended heavily on the quality of the company drinking the tea. Interesting conversation tended to result in cloudy fates, requiring a longer stay and another cup of tea. Conversely, a clear reading, either weal or woe it didn't matter, would see the visitor or visitors suddenly eager to find their fortune or prepare for a bitter encounter. This would see them out quickly.

The orc spent some time looking at the swirling tea while Auntie sipped. The flecks flowed in lazy circles. The patterns were predictable, but she only had minor control. She could orient the cup to change where the slower bits of tea would settle or move the cup to stir it into movement again, but she couldn't control the formation of patterns along the bottom.

Chicken drained his cup. "Read mine, Auntie." He held it out to her.

"It's the same as always, Chicken. It's some great destiny I can't make out clearly." She hadn't even looked inside.

The orc tried the tea. She found it pungent and somewhat intoxicating. Nonetheless, it left a delicate flowery aftertaste.

"I'm not an orc," the orc said suddenly.

She spoke to the cup, as though embarrassed, and tended to rub her palms together, as though drying them, or removing something sticky. The task required her utmost attention, making it seem very deliberate, before she resumed swirling her tea, alternating between the tasks at a regular cadence.

"I was exiled from my tribe for that crime," she said.

Chicken opened his mouth to ask the obvious question but was intercepted by Auntie.

"A terrible crime among your people, not being an orc."

"They're not my people," the orc said. It wasn't spoken impatiently or sarcastically, but as a fact freshly stated.

"Of course," Auntie said, "Please forgive us for being fearful. Orcs have a reputation, and my children are excitable."

The orc-thing seemed miles away to Chicken, but she said, "I know. I don't have a people I recognize. I don't know what it is to be one of me."

Chicken looked between her and Auntie, trying to gauge if his question was pertinent. He just asked it.

"So, what are you?"

He earned a look from Auntie, but no scolding. She must have wanted to know, too.

"I'm a cowbird."

The cowbird orc sipped her tea, as though there was nothing more to tell.

A flip at the entrance drew her attention and distracted her. She had turned just in time to see a kobold snout withdraw and the flap close.

"They're curious about you," Auntie said, undisturbed. "I'll admit I share in their curiosity. Do you have a name?"

The orc girl set the cup on the floor of the tent. The dry dirt gritted against the bottom of the cup as she twiddled it, turning it like a dial this way and that. Auntie could watch as her question was weighed.

"Penelope," the orc said eventually. She pronounced it like "pen" and "elope".

"Nice to meet you Penelope, I'm Chicken," said Chicken. "I'm glad you're not an orc after all."

"Why is that?"

"Orcs are scary."

She nodded, accepting his reasoning. She shared in the sentiment, despite, or perhaps because, of her upbringing. Orcs were powerful, in charge, and increasingly violent as a matter of pride, believing themselves to be the natural rulers of the world around them. It wasn't a world view to which Penelope subscribed.

"I'm afraid the others believe as Chicken does. We will have to work to convince them that you are not as you appear," Auntie said.

Penelope surprised them by asking, "Why?"

"Because if you'll be staying with us, they'll need to get used to you being around anyway."

Penelope nodded uncertainly, staring into her cup.

"Have you finished your tea yet?" Auntie asked, "Hand it over so I can read your fortune."

Penelope quickly finished it and held it out to the old kobold who impatiently palmed it.

"Let's see now," she said, peering into the cup. She made several thinking noises before saying, "That's odd. Chicken, hand me your cup."

He eagerly did so, and Auntie looked between one and the other.

"What is it?" Chicken asked, speaking for Penelope as well.

"You take a look," Auntie said. She sounded irritated.

She put both cups on the ground, careful not to disturb the contents, and the other two bent over to compare.

"Woah!" said Chicken.

Penelope was more skeptical. "What does it mean?"

"What do you mean? They look exactly the same."

Chapter 9 – Desert Queen

"What does it mean that our fortunes are the same, Auntie?" Chicken asked.The old kobold had seemed deep in thought for the time Penelope and Chicken studied their tea leaves. When the silence grew too much, he reached out to touch her. Auntie's eyes opened slowly and her eyes rolled down, the pupils orbiting to focus on him."Auntie, were you sleeping?""Don't be foolish," she replied, blinking several times. "I was communing with the spirits.What was the original question?""We were talking about why my and Penelope's tea leaves look the same.""Yes, I thought it was something like that.You and Penelope here simply have similar fates." Chicken scratched his head, making a rasping sound of claw on scale."You mean we're going to do the same thing?""It's tricky to say.You could end up working together accomplishing some goal," her voice trailed off and Chicken thought she had fallen asleep. She surprised him by continuing, "That's probably it, actually.You two are fated to work together towards that same great destiny your tea leaves are always telling me about."A small cough caught both of their attention. They looked at Penelope, a fist still covering her mouth.She started stutteringly, saying, "I'm not here for fate. Or destiny for that matter. I really appreciate your kindness. I'd like to repay you somehow, but-"Auntie didn't let her finish. Quickly the old kobold said, "You're very welcome, child. We're not finished with you, but since you mentioned it you have some time yet to find a way to repay us." For a moment, she cocked her head, then suddenly picked up the teacups and set them aside. "Let's put the future away for now. We've got the present to deal with. You haven't met anyone but myself and Chicken, and I think it's time you had some fresh air."Chicken sniffed before saying, "I smell cooking. They've probably got food ready.""Really?" Auntie said, bemused, "I hadn't noticed. Both of you help me up." She gestured to the two who were seated around her to get up, holding her arms out. Obediently, they did as she commanded."But your jar. Should I clean it up? It was my fault, really.""Oh, no. It's probably dry now, that stuff is quick. And that spot has probably never been cleaner. Come, eat with us." She got her legs and cane under her and strode to the door. The three of them stepped out into the rest of Very Small Numbers.Outside, the sun was almost touching the horizon. Shadows of the surrounding rock spires lay over the uneven encampment like strips of dark blanket. The sky had turned to interesting bruise-like colors."Shari is making locust and brown mold kibbeh." Auntie licked her scaly lips as the three of them came upon a fire pit. There, a greenish kobold was digging a wide, shallow covered pot out of embers at the edge of a moderate bonfire. Looking on with her, Penelope noticed, was a growing audience of hungry neighbors. She noticed also how they stared when they noticed her, moving respectfully out of her way as she followed Auntie. Or was it verging on fearfully?The idea of eating fungus and bugs didn't turn Penelope's stomach. She'd had more exotic foods before. What did make her feel uneasy was the growing smell of spice in the air. The dish, free of the coals, was unlidded, revealing palm sized lozenges of roasted food. They could have been meat patties for all Penelope could tell. Everyone there was served one of the patties, wrapped in a thin fabric. It all smelled like bitter, spicy licorice to Penelope. "Two for you, Penelope?" Auntie asked, taking a kibbeh from Shari. "Umm. I'll try one." Shari, startled, looked from Auntie to Penelope and back. "But Auntie-" she started to say. "Hush, dear. One more, please." Another was begrudgingly wrapped and handed from Shari to Auntie, and from Auntie to Penelope. Chicken was happily chewing his first bite. His mouth full, he said, "We had a blessing of locusts recently. Shari does a good job grinding up the legs and bits really small. Go on and try it, they're good." Encouraged, she held the meatball close for a sniff. Altogether, it didn't smell unappetizing. She decided to risk a bite. "No!" a voice cried. It hadn't come from the kibbeh. "What is it doing eating our food!?" The voice, it turned out, came from an irate and prickly looking kobold. It was pointing at Penelope from across the way. "Now, Salander, don't go making a fuss." This was Auntie, sitting on the edge of the fire pit, poised to savor the first bite of her dinner. "We've discussed this to death already." "A fuss?" the kobold Salander asked mockingly. "Oh, I'm just fussing about an orc among us." He marched over to Auntie and put his hands on his hips. "I hope you're not expecting to eat that. If it's eating tonight, it's eating your food." "I didn't mean-" Penelope started bashfully, but Auntie spoke over her. "Don't be ridiculous, Salander," she tittered, instantly shrinking his outrage into a temper tantrum, in the way only a maternal figure can. She took a bite of her kibbeh. "Honestly. You can't expect me to believe we can't spare a little food and water."Salander fumed, grinding his teeth as he stood over her. With restraint, he said, "Auntie. You are not in charge here."She chewed silently in response, neither affirming or denying.Salander continued, "So if I say we can't have an orc here, if I say it's not eating our food, then we're not.""It's ok," Chicken said cheerily, "she's not an orc, Salander."This earned him a cold glare from Salander. Luckily for Chicken, it bounced off his exorbitant obliviousness."Penelope," Auntie said, at once dismissing and undermining Salander, "come over here and sit next to me." She patted the seat next to her. As she neared, Salander watched, eventually looking up at the orc figure that towered over him. He recoiled as she made a sudden move, which was just her sitting down next to Auntie.

"You may have forgotten in your senility," he said in a low voice, "but orcs are not our friends, Auntie." Penelope noticed some of the kobold neighbors shuffling awkwardly away, clearly affected by his words. She could see Salander notice this too, as he smirked slightly. Pithy came to sit by Penelope. Then Chicken, having finished his dinner. Then a few kobolds Penelope didn't recognize.Salander's smirk wavered.Things cascaded into a movement among the others, and eventually the pit was ringed with kobolds and one orc-looking girl. Some of these were the skeptical shufflers."I think it's time for a story," Auntie said, looking at everyone except Salander. He threw his hands in the air."Fine. You win." He walked in a frustrated circle before stabbing a finger at the old kobold. "But when this snake bites us, it's on you. The raiding. The imprisonment. The bloodshed. Her people are going to find us, and it'll be because you took her in.""Tonight, I think it'll be the story of Hare and the Sand Adder."Salander stormed off, and Auntie continued."Once upon a time, long long ago, the wastes east of the mountains, our home, was very different. The land was young and life was new, and the desert wasn't a desert but green with plants. This was ideal for Hare, who ate the grasses that grew here. They were plentiful in those days, along with beasts of the hunt and tasty bugs and green bushes and water. It ran through the fields, wild as anything else. The animals of the land east of the mountains were happy, and most important of all, the Great Kobold was happy. And so things went until the rain stopped."The Great Kobold, as kobolds were the biggest and strongest back then, was queen of the land. All the animals were scared of her sharp teeth, her powerful intelligence, and most of all, her large wings which bore her aloft so that she could watch the animals from above. No one noticed much that the rain stopped coming, but as it went on, the plants became withered and thirsty and the watering holes became smaller. The Great Kobold noticed when her mirror pond could no longer show her full majesty."She immediately sent for Hare, cleverest of the animals. He who escaped Hyena by telling jokes, giving her her laugh. Hare who convinced Grasshopper Mouse he's a hunter, putting bravery enough in the little mouse's heart to hunt snakes. When he received word of the summons, he said to himself, 'She will want me to do something dangerous, or else she would do it herself. I must outsmart her or she will not reward me.' Determined to profit, whatever the endeavor, he went to the queen. Now, Hare had never met the queen before, but he had heard about her. When she received him, he saw she was big, big, big!" Auntie grew louder with each "big", startling the younger kobolds.

Speaking the queen's part, she growled, "The queen said to Hare, 'The rain has stopped. The plants and animals are thirsty. My mirror pool has dried up. I want you to send a message to Stormhaegen in the heavens above to send rain to me and my people. Will you do this for me?' Hare, scared as he was, boldly asked the queen, 'This is a dangerous task for someone so small and weak. Why not send Water Buffalo or Mountain Lion? They are bigger and stronger than me.'" Auntie wheedled Hare's part, making the young kobolds laugh. Penelope looked to Chicken, confused.

Chicken, veteran story listener, whispered to her that Hare was already a legendary hero, if the other stories about him were anything to go by. Auntie, ignoring them, continued, "The queen saw Hare, small and fragile compared to her, and said, 'This is true. You are not the biggest and strongest. I summoned you for this task because you are the swiftest and cleverest. I want rain, and I am not willing to wait.' Hare replied, 'I can do this thing for you.' This pleased the queen, but Hare continued, 'but I will request payment for this dangerous task.' The queen was very wealthy in shiny gold, food, and drink. Knowing Hare desired her wealth she roared, 'You are after my gold! Go now and do as I say! If you fail, I will eat you!'" Auntie really shouted this time. She wailed with the queen's wrath into the night sky. Penelope found she was impressed, despite herself. "Hare fled, dodging her powerful jaws, and left to deliver the message to Stormhaegen in his cloud throne among the heavens." At this point in the story, she stopped for a while. She ate her food, another kibbeh kindly brought to her by one of the youngsters. A kobold raised her hand. "Did the queen eat Hare?" She was jostled by her neighbor, who answered her question. "Don't be dumb. He always gets out of trouble." She retorted, "He didn't bring the rain back, though. It's not like in Auntie's story now, is it?" He didn't have an answer to that one. "We'll have to wait until tomorrow night to find out, won't we? It's time all kobolds be sleeping or keeping watch." The circle dissolved and the fire was lessened.

Chapter 10 - Serpent and Sea-Legs

Below decks on the ship The Hereafter, Trevor Tweesly sat at the navigator's desk. Beside him was a porthole through which he could see the tilting, churning horizon. At least, he could if it were daylight outside.

He pored over his notes and star charts by the light of a nearly spent candle in the holder, which was bolted to the desk top to keep from tipping or sliding as the room's gravity swayed indecisively. The pieces of yellowing parchment which he was studying were in varying states of being rolled up, and each depicted the curved lines and dots which are the hallmark of the navigator's craft.

They were each depictions of a night sky, like a an insect on a collector's board, euthanized, with the wings spread and the body pinned amidst descriptive notes.

Trevor, in between the furious action of his quill, would pause to push his round iron-rimmed spectacles back up the bridge of his nose before resuming his organized scribbling.

The small room was illuminated with an inpatient flickering light, threatening to go out, sputtering indignantly against the humid, salty air.

Strung up along the far wall was a hammock. It lay twisted and tangled, neglected and unkempt.

A blanket and pillow were caught in the webbing, not unlike the husk of a fly in an abandoned cobweb.

A bronze sextant on a tripod stared limply down at the floor.

Mounds of things sat against the other walls, like hounds haunching at the edge of campfire light. They were bags, crates, canvas, lumber, rope, and a small bookshelf with tomes.

The books on the bookshelf were locked into place with clasping Iron bars, restrained from gravity's seductive dance. They were too delicate and valuable to be left free to the elements, so they were kept apart for their own safety.

The skinny brown haired man, his thoughts at the end of their track, slowed his scribbling.

The fine details trickled out of his brain, down through his arm, and he trapped the final notes of the ship's route there on the page.

Satisfied, he holstered his quill and stoppered the ink well, both built into the desk.

He folded his pair of compasses and put them back into their velvet fold, which he rolled up and secreted into the drawer, along with his leather-sheathed quill knife. This he did with care, obvious even through the hallmarks of sleep deprivation.

After blotting the ink from the finished work, he stacked the notes into a rough sheaf before laying them into a binder.

Finally, eagerly, he rolled up the topmost charts on the desk. He slid the roll into a waterproof scroll holder with the cap dated for this week in a practical script. This he deposited into its place among the pigeonholes on the wall, one in a collection of sixty three others.

Standing there with the binder under his arm and about to go out the door, he stopped to glance at the hammock.

He stood there for several seconds, trapped in a kind of trance. For Tweesly, the room fell away.

The weight of the binder in his arm disappeared.

The gentle swaying of the ship became the pulse of his universe.

He stopped noticing the flickering light.

In that moment, he saw only the essence of the hammock.

Tearing himself away from his thoughts, he extinguished the candle, which was mere minutes away from burning out on its own.

The firelight was replaced with the grey light of dawn, which had just begun creeping from the horizon.

This pre-dawn light inched over the ocean. It crawled through the port hole and into Trevor's room.

But it had just missed him.

The navigator's robes fluttered gracelessly as he opened the door and left his meager quarters.

It was time to report their route into the east.

****

Trevor stumbled on his land-legs, through sleeplessness, and across the deck of the Hereafter.

He was aiming for the captain's quarters. He needed to give his report to the captain before the information evaporated out his ears and into the sky.

Only with his message deposited safely could he return to his room and sleep until the next night.

When he woke up, it would a new night with different stars.

A ship had very little chance of getting anywhere without a navigator versed in the sequence of the night skies. Hundreds of zodiacs, a new one every night, were memorized by capable navigators.

A new guiding star would rise every time the sun set.

Without the knowledge bound in Tweesly's books, the crew would be utterly lost.

Gods help them if they were out further than they could see the shore, adrift on the shifting currents, or freshly emerged from a storm.

But their ship is freed from such a fate so long as Tweesly and his tools of the trade are onboard.

Their voyage's origin lay to the north, in the oversized harbor hosting most of the region's commerce. Much trade occurred there among the underwater cities, pontoon villages, cliff outposts, and docks at the woods edge.

The Hereafter was abandoning the safety of the harbor.

A venture sought by the captain has drawn the crew away even from where most thieves and pirates frequented.

Their journey pulled them away from sight of the shore.

The ship bucked unexpectedly, leaving Tweesly in a split. The drop then sent him to the floor.

Luckily, he rescued his binder.

Deciding against rash action, he lay on his back, mustering his meager strength.

Steadying himself against a bound barrel, he fought the rolling ground beneath him, working half pace for a bit before growing nauseous from staring at his feet.

He began to mumble and groan, a more agreeable alternative to giving up.

"Heavens, lad, where are you going in a hurry?"

Tweesly looked around and noticed a dwarf. The ship's cook, he remembered.

He was sitting on a spool of rope and looking at Tweesly with the usual concern, Tweesly being the runt of the litter back home.

"Why doncha sit down and take a break? You can hug that bucket over there for a bit." He gestured with his whittling knife at a waterproofed bucket which had otherwise blended into the scenery.

Tweesly wanted to thank him, but he just did what the dwarf suggested without a word.

He ended up sitting cross legged, holding the bucket with his knees. It was moist and sticky on the outside, and as big as his torso. The morning light gently gathered on the surface of whatever liquid it contained.

"On behalf o' the crew, welcome aboard The Hereafter," the dwarf said, waving his arms expansively. "It's the promised land, where y'can work a' much a' you like, where there's a' much food an' drink a' y'can stomach, an' the people here ain' half bad neither."

In a quieter voice he added, "It's the best bit o' life before Eternity, believe you me." Trever could not discern any lie.

The rest of the crew called the cook Cookie, and aside from the mediocre fare, Tweesly knew nothing more about him.

Cookie was in his usual grease stained apron, wearing his slightly drooping chef's hat.

Trevor wondered briefly if a hat like that was a requirement for the chef, but was interrupted by a sudden deposit he made in the bucket.

"Don' worry about that," Cookie said sympathetically, "It'll pass."

More brightly he said, "Breakfast is ready, so you can replace whatchu lose when you can."

While he had been reassuring Tweesly with his words, he hadn't been looking at him.

Instead, he was concentrating at a thing in his hands. He was whittling something with a small knife, casting the shavings haphazardly on the ground.

Trevor found it eased his nausea to focus on the strange shavings. The slight noise the knife made as it cut through the material was unfamiliar to Trevor, quieter, and, in the moments of silence between the slices, he realized it was soap.

The dwarf's deft hands were turning a bar of soap into a little statue of a person.

The object was too small and too far away for Trevor to see details.

"Wood is at a premium out on the ocean," Cookie said, picking up on Trevor's stare, "Besides, I wouldn' wanna get my hands dir-"

Tweesly suddenly felt the sensation of falling. Cookie felt it too, and it had cut him off mid-sentence.

The moment passed when he hit the deck rear-first and almost toppled. The bucket still in his grip, he successfully made another deposit.

The dwarf, returning to his whittling, said, "Random wave. Some are bigger than others. The ship rides them up and up like a plateau, then smacks down." He clapped his hands for emphasis on the smack.

"You ge' used to it, like the rest."

More silence welled between them, punctuated by Tweesly's nausea.

Deciding he could wait no longer, he stood up.

Despite his swimming head, he lifted the bucket to the side. Cookie called out to stop him.

"Wha' are you doing? Leave it. It's swab water. It won' make any difference with some sick in it. The swabbie ain' got any more."

Tweesly shrugged and went to put the bucket down.

It slid away from him.

Tweesly noticed the deck getting steeper and steeper.

He braced for the fall and the slap, but when it didn't come, he opened his eyes.

Cookie had a bewildered look.

"This ain' no wave."

Beside the ship, the water roiled.

Cookie sounded the alarm, which consisted of running below decks while screaming incoherently.

Trevor's eyes went to his binder, which was also sliding away towards the prow of the ship.

The ship creaked and groaned as it was flexed in unintended ways, one end gradually leaving the water.

Trevor stumble-ran to catch his binder, single-minded.

It wouldn't save them, but the activity gave him purpose.

The crew bubbled up from below decks in various states of sleep and panic.

Several people crossed between Trevor and his binder, largely ignoring both, buffeting each as they passed.

Across the ship came chaotic cries.

"Something's got us!"

"Raise the sail!"

"To arms!"

"I didn't hear no cannons!"

"Some guts-for-brains really snarled this rope!"

It all died away, causing Trevor to look up from his fleeing book.

The roil by the ship had disappeared.

In its place there was a great serpent head.

It extended from the water, continuing up and up, towering over the ship.

While he wasn't looking, Trevor's binder had hit a wall and stopped.

Trevor himself lost his footing nearing the end of the chase and also hit a wall and stopped, head first beside the book.

Next to him, a door opened. It was the door he had been aiming for. The door to the captain's quarters.

From inside strode a minotaur.

Trevor, being close to the ground at the time, first saw the translucent, faceted hooves at the ends of its furry legs.

He looked up further.

The minotaur wore stately garments, befitting an officer of a ship, and strands of jewelry bound around his great horns.

The minotaur ascended the inclined deck with grace for several paces, stirring a wake of murmurs among the crew with his passage.

The great serpentine head looked down at the ship.

The sea snake, the only description befitting this monster that Trevor could think of, was wholly covered with pearly white scales, right up to its head.

Its head, however, was adorned with a dark blue crest, like a gnarled face mask made of horn.

Only its green eyes could be seen through the holes in the crest, but only by what poor creature the serpent was looking at.

Looking at it, and its terrible immensity, Trevor wished he had kept the bucket.

The now assembled crew, armed with all manner of bladed weapons and improvised clubs, awaited orders from the minotaur.

Having reached the edge nearest the serpent, he stood commandingly, his hands behind his back.

The serpent hissed like whale exhaust, showing its many pointed teeth.

The minotaur boomed, "Serpent! What business have you with us!"

To the nearest crewman, in a calm voice, he ordered that the barrels bound on the deck be uncovered.

The serpent replied without moving its jaw, the words slithering out unimpeded.

"Identify yourself, vessel. We recognize your make, but not your crew. You are in our waters, and we demand tribute."

The minotaur shouted back, "We do not carry anything in your waters save for our lives and materials for sustainment!"

The serpent listened silently.

The minotaur continued, "It is not the way of your people to demand more than a quarter of trade goods, and we have none! Look, these barrels are empty and we sit high on the water, at least until your arrival!"

He gestured to the empty barrels as he said this.

"Why do you travel, elf ship, if not for profit?"

"This is our own business! You have no right to inquire!"

By this point in the proceedings, Trevor had righted himself and claimed the binder.

Strangely, he felt no need for a bucket, though he would need a change of pants later.

Keeping his eyes on the serpent towering over the ship, he crawled up behind a halfling, who looked equally engrossed.

"What's going on? Why aren't we dead yet?" Trevor hissed at the halfling.

Too shocked to be startled, the halfling droned, "Payment must be made to the lord of the open oceans, the white serpent of the exterior water ways."

"That at least explains the banter. Why have I never heard of this?"

"All seafaring people make agreements when they first try to leave for new lands by boat. It's ancient history consigned to myth." The halfling shrugged.

"Very informative, and better spoken than I expected."

"Thank you. My brother and I were performers in another life." His face screwed up like he tasted something bitter. "I hope I don't have to start thinking about the next one."

The minotaur and the serpent concluded discussions, resulting in the serpent receding into the water.

The minotaur demanded that the barrels be covered again, and the halfling who had been speaking to Trevor hopped-to.

Following that came more orders.

The cannons were to be inspected, the deck to be swabbed, the sails to be somesuch or another.

The terminology escaped Trevor long before the final command was issued. The ship was suddenly lively.

The minotaur returned to the door by which Trevor stood, and offering the binder he said, "Navigation complete, captain."

The minotaur laughed, "Captain? No, Mr. Tweesly. Did you not meet the captain when you joined our crew?" Trevor shook his head.

"Come, then. I am First Mate Gorestomp. I'll introduce you."

He opened the door and gestured Tweesly to enter.

"Mr. Tweesly. The captain of The Hereafter."

Chapter 11 - Betrayal

Dawn spread its long bright fingers over the wasteland, groping for each living thing there. When it found Very Small Numbers, Chicken was already awake and moving.

"Penelope!" he called, walking among the huts and lodges. "Penelope!"

She hadn't been at the waiting spot, and he wondered briefly if he should have told her ahead of time where that had been. In any case, he had to find her soon if she was to join him. His feet drew him towards Auntie's tent, the grand high Knower of Things. He found the hut inert and sleepy. Auntie was not a morning kobold, as the rest of the village well-knew. Looking for Penelope here would be done at his own peril. He pushed back the flap cautiously, illuminating the room a little at a time.

At first, he sent just a spear of dull grey morning light, pushing the flap aside only a little. He saw only hanging dry ingredients and a dirt floor. He widened the gap, spilling more light into the room.

"Penelope?" he whispered, worried someone inside would hear him.

He saw pots and tubs, but no sign of life. If he pressed further, it increased his chance of waking Auntie. But he needed to find Penelope, so he steeled himself and drew the flap further aside.

Something grabbed his elbow causing him to yelp and turn around.

"It's a good morning, Chicken," someone said.

The someone happened to be Pithy. "Do you need something from Auntie?" she asked. She seemed oblivious to her having just caused Chicken to jump out of his scales.

She continued, "You usually leave before daylight. Did you forget something and have to come back?"

"I'm looking for Penelope," he whispered. "We'd planned for her to come with me."

"Salander is letting her go with you?" the young kobold asked, tilting her head.

"He hasn't given her permission to do anything since she arrived," Chicken said irritably, "But I'm sure he'd be ecstatic to find she's gone." He crossed his arms.

"Ecstatic to find who's gone?" a voice said behind him.

****

Penelope was sitting in front of a thing she was rubbing with a stone. It made prolonged ssshhk ssshhk noises as she drew the stone along the length of the thing. Laid out beside her on a crude mat were a variety of other stones, all roughly hand-sized, and small bowls each filled with some liquid or gel. She was sitting in the shade of a rock out of sight of the village as she worked. The thing before her was long, thin, and intermittently shiny grey and rough red. She had secured it on its back, insomuch as a thing like this could have a back, with its leading edge pointing towards the cloudless sky.

It had been some time since Penelope had taken up residence in Very Small Numbers. She used the moment and dull repetitive task to reflect on her stay.

Her verdict was that this place was alien to her.

Sure, she could speak the language and eat the food, but the kobolds were different from her own people. They were primitive. There was not a single prisoner among them to perform labor. In the few weeks she had been with them, they had only gone on a single hunt. When they returned with only one slain beast, they rejoiced. They aided one another without contest, where her own people bred strength in their numbers by doing the opposite.

The orc girl sat in the shade, her arm drawing the rock from one end to the other, picking it up, and starting again. The rough red gradually flaked away, showing more shiny grey in its place.

She felt the understanding click into place. These kobolds screamed weakness to her. Where her people struggled against each other to claw their way to the top social and physical standing, these kobolds provided for one another, doing the work so another would benefit. And now they had included her in their debauchery. Don't they understand, like she did, that you don't get something from nothing?

She would have to show them a new way. A way that would work.

The noises stopped as she paused to consider her next move, which was to nod and put the rock on the mat. She wet her thumb in a bowl and rubbed it over one of the other rocks present before selecting it and returning to her task. Slowly the new rock was drawn over the thing in front of her.

ssshhk...ssshhk...ssshhk

****

Chicken turned around to see who had spoken. Salander stood with his fists on his hips.

While Chicken babbled, unable to form words, Pithy said sternly, "We're talking about Penelope. Chicken's right. You've been making it hard on her since she got here."

He made a sour face. "And how exactly have I been making it difficult for the orc?" This question he directed at Chicken, who was still floundering.

"You accused her of thieving," Pithy said.

Salander scoffed. "I did no such thing."

"Yes you did! You set up those new cubby rules and everything when Oreson said that rock-moving stick was missing."

"Well, yes, I did, but when things start disappearing-"

"You said we had to mark our cubbies with one of our own scales. Penelope can't have a cubby because she doesn't have scales!"

"That was an oversight," Salander snapped. "Anyway, I didn't actually say it was the orc's doing."

Under his breath, Chicken said, "You might as well have." Then he saw Salander's eyes narrow, apparently having heard him.

"I can't believe you two. After all I've done for this orc already, and here you are acting like it's one of us."

"All you've done? Since when do you do anything, Salander? You stalk around the camp and boss us around. Move this, shuck that, knap these." Chicken looked at Pithy, surprised at her rant.

Salander's eyes had grown wide, too. "Maybe put in some work first, then you can complain about what we're doing for Penelope."

Salander crossed his arms and looked at her like a herpetologist discovering a rare and venomous species of snake that had suddenly appeared in his living room.

"I don't have to stand for this," he said quietly before walking off. He stopped and turned back. "None of you know the danger that orc poses to our community, but I'm doing something about it." And with that he left.

Chicken and Pithy stood in silence as the morning light gathered around them.

"What do you think he meant by that?" Chicken said finally.

"Maybe he did something already and that's why we can't find Penelope!" Pithy said, sudden worry in her voice.

Chicken crossed his arms and thought. "No, because he didn't know she was missing. He acted like someone making a plan, not having just gone through with a plan."

The flap to the tent came back and a horrific monster appeared, with gimlet eyes and sharp teeth.

"Stop arguing outside my tent!" it said. The monster was Auntie. She saw it was Chicken and Pithy, which gave her enough pause for the sleep to creep back into her. She groaned. "It's light already?" she said, rubbing her eyes.

"Auntie, do you know where Penelope is?" Chicken asked quickly.

"Hrm? Penelope?" She blinked a few times and coughed. "She woke me up earlier, picking up her goblin sword and kit. I think she went out over yon ridge to clean it."

Chicken looked in the direction she indicated. A path wound up behind a wall of rock on one edge of the village. "Thanks Auntie!"

"Have fun scavenging. I'm going back to sleep," she said with a tired slur before returning to the dark. Chicken went off to find his mentee.

She was coming down the path when he got there. A sword hung from her belt as she carried a rolled up mat.

"Chicken," she said when she saw him. It was said neither happily nor coldly, merely in acknowledgement. He had come to accept that this was merely her way.

"We've got to go," he said, failing to keep impatience out of his tone.

"I need to put up the blade sharpening kit. I will only be a moment going to Auntie's."

"There's no time. The herd is going to pass us by before we can get out there. My cubby's on the way out, you can leave it with me."

"Are you sure? If I'm caught pulling it out of your cubby later, I'll get in trouble. Like when Shrub took that pouch of sling bullets from Jonesy."

"I'll make sure you won't. I was just talking with Salander about how dumb his new rule is."

"Dumb or not, I'm not going to break it. You'll need to get it out for me next time I want to do more sharpening."

"Yes, ok. Let's hurry."

Before long, they were at Chicken's cubby. It was a small hole in the rock, just big enough for two hands, and just above it, embedded in the rock, was one of Chicken's scales.

"I'll stand over here while you work," Penelope said, holding out the roll. Chicken took it and set it aside the hole. He reached into the cubby and took out a small carved container, a handful of fist-sized quartz gems, and a large mushroom. He put the sharpening kit inside, and then returned the other items before dusting off his hands and standing up.

"Alright, let's go," he said, but then pointed at her waist. "You won't need that. Do you want to leave it too?"

Penelope looked horrified.

"I-... I think I'll keep it all the same," she said curtly.

Chicken shrugged in consent. He also shrugged off a densely woven wicker backpack, one of the two he had strapped to him, and handed it to her. "You'll need this."

She held it up and looked inside. There was a bundle of light leather. When she pulled it out, it turned out to be two leather bags.

"What's this?" she asked.

"You'll need it," he said again. "Best to carry the bags in the backpack until we're headed back." He started walking away from the village.

She stuffed the bags back inside, swung the pack onto her back, and followed.

Trekking through the wastelands was much less a leisurely walk than it was a horizontal rock-climb. Chicken and Penelope strode, clambered, strafed, hopped, teetered, and toddled their way in a roughly southerly direction. Neither spoke as they travelled, Chicken for lack of habit, always scavenging alone, and Penelope for a very different reason. He noticed how stiffly she moved, out in the wilderness. Not in an unskilled way, but cautiously, like she was expecting something unpleasant.

Once, a rock had bounced weird, making a distinct noise. Penelope's hand had gone immediately to her sword and had almost drawn it. As quickly as she had reacted, she had simply gone back to climbing.

Even when they had stopped for a meal, which Chicken had been carrying in his own pack, she seemed almost nervous.

He peeled an egg and stuffed it in his mouth, saying, "I like your enthusiasm. It'll keep you safe on the more dangerous trails."

It was at that moment that something stirred behind them. Penelope drew her sword and whirled. She held her foe in stunned silence. Its nose twitched.

"It's just a hippity hop," Chicken said. It was enough to break whatever spell had been placed over the small camp and the floppy-eared rodent bounded away.

Penelope sat down, not even watching it as it ran away. "I feel this trail is treacherous enough. I keep waiting for your test, but it never comes.

"My test?" Chicken said through another mouthful of egg.

"The reason to bring me out here." She seemed shocked. "You had some reason to bring me along. When you told me I wouldn't need my weapon, I feared you would require me to take down our quarry with my bare hands. I feel ashamed to have brought a weapon."

Chicken swallowed. "I had figured you brought it for protection, but this trail is too tricky for howlers and too open for prowlers. Howlers like flat ground for a turn of speed."

Thoughts clicked into place for Penelope, and her horrified look returned. "We must seek something truly abominable, then." She shook the fear off and said haltingly, "I-... I will do my best. We will exalt in their blood."

Chicken tossed something to Penelope, who caught it on impulse. It was the last boiled egg.

"If there's blood in what we're after, we've got bigger problems," he said. "We're after those." He pointed off in the direction of some flat land. Several lumbering shapes were crawling along the horizon. Herd beasts.

Penelope watched them in silence before turning to Chicken.

"We're not after the howlers or prowlers?"

Chicken shook his head.

"We're not... charging those things?"

"Are you crazy? We could get killed doing that."

Penelope sat down, processing what he had been telling her . It was completely alien to her, like it had descended from above in a hub cap and stepped out to show off its splotchy skin and eye-stalks. She allowed the relief to take over.

"Thank Ogg," she said as the tension ran out. "I thought it was like one of father's hunts. Having avoided those for so long I guess I expected it here."

"Would you really have attacked those herd beasts if I asked?"

She met his gaze and said, "For you? Unflinchingly."

"Would you do something worse?"

She looked perplexed. "Worse?"

He pointed out at the beasts again. "That's what we're here for. Grass eaters make a lot of it."

"What? I don't see it. All I can see is where they've trampled and-..." It took only a moment for her to pick up on what he was saying. She made a face.

"It's good fuel for the fire, and why we have the bags and backpacks. We'll have to cover our scent to get close enough."

"Cover our scent with what?"

He gave her a look.

"Oh."

****

Penelope and Chicken crept back into Very Small Numbers in a dingy haze, their packs and bags full. They off-loaded at the fire.

"There's nobody here," Penelope said. It was true. The village was empty.

"Maybe they're just avoiding us." He gestured at the fuel they had gathered. "Auntie will know what's going on." He rubbed himself down with some loose and gritty dirt from the extinguished fire before heading to her hut.

Pulling the flap aside, he entered. "Auntie, where is-..." Once inside, Chicken saw Auntie and Salander. They were on their knees with their hands behind their backs. They had gags on.

"You're back," a voice said behind them. A deep, male orc voice.

Chapter 12 - Standoff

Imagine a dark place. A dark place with the smell of dust and mold and water. The rocks here silently converse about their crazy days when they were molten. When they were loose and free. When they mingled. It wasn't like that now. Everyone had settled since then, and all that was left for them of those hot, steamy, youthful days were memories. It was peaceful now. Respectable. No major upsets in at least a couple thousand years. The rocks remembered that, too. A great slam from above had rattled their neighborhood. It had been quite upsetting, and it was still a point of contention among them. But peace had returned quickly and the complaints faded. There wasn't much for it. For those thousands of years the rocks were left with their memories. And the new folks, the ones that appeared after the upheaval. Now, a new rowdiness was slowly building from those, geologically speaking, new arrivals. A faint glow, visible only in this complete darkness, pulsated a gentle blue, distressing the rocks with the hubbub. A mind turned over in its grave.

****

"Hey," the orc voice said, "You're Skullcrush, aren't you?"

Penelope regarded the squatting orcs. One was Marrowcrack and the other was Bloodboil. Fearfully, she drew her goblin sword, and the Marrowcrack laughed. "Not here, not here," he said mirthfully, "We don't do that no more. What, you think I'd be just hanging around with a Bloodboil? It's different now." This gave her pause.

The other orc nudged his companion. "Wait, if she's Skullcrush... I thought Lord Kairon beat old Justafar just last year."

In the confusion, Chicken ran to Auntie, who was tied up and gagged in the tent along with Salander.

"Yeah? And?" The Marrowcrack got up and idly ambled over to Chicken. The orc caught him by the shoulder before he could draw his dagger and cut her bonds. With the skill of a corn husker, he disarmed the kobold and tied him up with a length of rope.

The Bloodboil continued, "How wouldn't she know, then?" The Marrowcrack gave this some consideration.

"You've been out here hunting since then, right?" he asked Penelope.

Chicken and Penelope shared a glance. In the moment, her brain caught up with current events. She gave him a look she thought would tell him to trust her.

"Umm..Yeah. That's right."

"Been doin' the rite of the nameless god, then?"

The rite of the nameless god involved living naked in the wilderness for months at a time. It was a good way for lesser orcs to cut loose and build respect among peers.

"Yup. That's me," Penelope said with feigned certainty. Satisfied, the Marrowcrack gave the Bloodboil a smug look.

"Well, that's all fine, then," he said. "We got word from this one," the Marrowcrack pointed to Salander, "that you were here. You ain't been doing a good job imprisoning 'em." He sounded like a teacher chastising a below-average student.

Penelope gave a pained look at Chicken, saying, "I was getting around to it."

The two orcs each picked up a kobold. "Well, you take this one," the Marrowcrack said, gesturing to Chicken, "and we'll check on how the goblins are doing. We gotta head back to Hurraggh in the morning." The two dipped under the door of the bivouac.

Chicken hissed a whisper. "What was that?"

"I'm sorry, I'm sorry," she said hastily while kneeling down to examine his ropes, "but I think I know how I can get you out of this. Can you play along until then?"

"Why did he say Salander did this? Oh, Auntie," he moaned. Penelope shushed him to no avail.

"Chicken, you have to trust me. They'll kill you otherwise, and without a moment's thought," and then added, "They may even kill Auntie."

Chicken's blood froze at the thought. "Ok, alright," he said. It didn't make him feel better in the least, but he could keep it together for Auntie's sake.

"There's a lot going on I don't understand, but I'm doing my best," Penelope explained. "They're not of my clan, so they don't know I'm a Not-An-Orc. We can use that, at least until we encounter any Skullcrush." She stopped to think about what had been bugging her. "Usually, if you get any Skullcrush, Marrowcrack, or Bloodboil together, we'd fight to the death. I wonder what happened."

Chicken added, "Did he say they don't do that any more?"

"We're not dead now, so let's just keep going. Here, I'll carry you out like they told me."

With Chicken over her shoulder and the makings of a plan budding, she stepped outside. There, a commotion had picked up. Goblins were milling about the tents and bivouacs, herding bound kobolds, scavenging, and smashing. The kobolds were being tied together in the center of the village and being sat down. Auntie was set down among them, but the orcs kept Salander. Penelope caught them saying, "This one gets special treatment."

When Penelope went to set Chicken down with the rest of the kobolds, she found all of their eyes on her. They looked up at her with expectant faces. No, wait, it wasn't her. They were looking at Chicken. Pithy whispered, "You can do it Chicken."

Light dawned for him. He had the power, after all. The crowd urged him silently in their restraints, and he in turn felt empowered. He could do it. They didn't need Penelope to plot on their behalf. He could really do it to save them from these orcs. Penelope was confused, feeling left out of the loop. She looked to Auntie for guidance, but the old kobold was out cold from the stress.

"Cut my ropes, Penelope," he whispered to her.

"What? Why? What's going on?" she whispered back.

"I need you to trust me."

This gave her pause. Was there something she was missing? Some vital piece of information? What did these kobolds know? Could she afford sacrificing this tenuous charade with the interlopers?

Her hands held his restraints, motionless, as she looked in his eyes for answers. She snapped the cord with a pained expression that had nothing to do with the effort. He thanked her and scrambled away.

She whispered to Pithy, "What is he going to do?"

Her eyes glittered with hope and whispered back, "He told us before, lots of times. Chicken has natural magic."

To play it safe, Penelope kept by the kobolds amidst the goblins' shattering spree.

A few moments later, the two male orcs looked up at a kobold standing above them on a rock. One pointed and started to shout, "Hey, gobbos! You missed one!" but Chicken boomed, "Stop what you are doing, you filthy orcs and goblins!" He pointed a claw at the two orcs. One was sitting on a tent like a hammock seat and the other had just stood up from sitting on the ground.

"Yeah? Or what?" said the orc. Half the goblins had heeded Chicken and looked up at him. The other half were oblivious.

"If you will not stop," Chicken replied, pausing for dramatic effect, "then I will be forced to use magic on you."

The orc didn't guffaw. He didn't scream or cry, either. He stood there in defiance of Chicken. Only a few goblins were surprised by this. They'd been there when a kobold had blown up one of their own. The orc just frowned.

"Do it then," he said.

"What?"

"Blow us up. Do it." The other added, "If you can, you should."

This staggered Chicken for a second, but he regained his poise quickly. "This is your last warning."

"No it isn't." The other added, "Yeah, our last warning was when you told us to stop. Now you're just putting off the work."

Chicken took offense at this. These two, sitting calmly amidst the growing chaos of panicking goblins, defied his abilities.

"On the count of three!" he shouted, redoubling the effort of his pointed claw.

"Just do it!" the orc shouted as it kicked a passing goblin. He mumbled something to it as it lay on the ground.

"One!" shouted Chicken, as doubt creeped into his mind.

The orcs started ignoring him.

"Two!"

He didn't notice the squad of goblins had grown less messy and fewer in number.

"Three!" and as he shouted, he was tackled down by the sneaking goblins behind him. They tied him back up and dragged him down before the orcs. Penelope tried to hide her face in her hands without the other orcs seeing.

"Lesser races," the orc spat. He regarded Chicken. "Couldn't do it? Didn't have the nerve."

The other one said, "Kairon told us to be on the lookout for-"

"Shut up! How did this one get out, anyway?"

"Wasn't that the one the Skullcrush brought in? You tied that one up."

"You sayin' my shackling isn't good enough? Those were good knots and good rope."

The other just snorted.

"You do it then," and threw the rope at him. "I'm going to sleep."

As Penelope and the Bloodboil started wrangling goblins, one had made his way rather far from the camp. He hadn't seen the whole affair with Chicken, and was digging in a few suspect nooks in the rocks when he hit pay dirt. Out of the cubby he pulled several strange items. One was a wrapped bowl that contained some tasty ant larvae, which he ate. They were dead and a little stale, just like he liked them.

There was also a shiny rock, which he pocketed. At the very back, he touched something fleshy, and he pulled back. He tried again. It didn't struggle or bite him, so he took hold. He pulled out the mushroom. The goblin squealed with delight. He thought it had been gone forever! Looking around, he stashed it in his chef's hat and continued rooting about.

"You there!" the Bloodboil shouted, "You ain't leaving! Get back here!" With no more food and no water, he drudged back to the orcs for the night.

****

Out in the wastelands, a kobold was looking down at his own body.

"Shrub," came a voice from behind him, "you are dead." It said it with the blunt force of a textbook swatting a fly.

After what he and his companion had been through, he didn't turn around. He just said sadly, "I didn't know they'd spotted us."

The voice behind him listened.

"We were trailing them. Oreson said we could stay just out of reach and lead them back to camp." He said this sadly, as well, but there were no tears.

"It didn't work out that way."

The kobold sniffled. "He didn't deserve to suffer like that."

"Neither of you did."

"And now those monsters know where camp is."

He imagined the voice nodding. "Would you like to know how it ends?"

Shrub shook his head. "I can guess."

"Are you sure? You might be pleasantly surprised," the voice tempted, "Oreson was." A new voice, a recognizable voice, said, "It's not what you think."

Shrub turned around to see an old woman, sitting on an invisible chair and holding a smoking white stick between her fingers. Oreson was standing beside her, holding a cookie.

This time, the tears came.

Chapter 13 - Instruction

"Do you all know what this is?" The gate guard held up a horn for the gate drivers to see. The group stared blankly at it with slack jaws and glazed eyes.

"No answers? Did anyone come here today with their thinker? I'll tell you what it is. This horn here is what I blow when someone needs to come through that gate there." He pointed at the massive stone doors, currently shut, with teams of prisoners rigged to each by long harnesses. "Would you like me to show you what it sounds like? Do you think you remember?"

One of the drivers picked his nose, clenching the handle of his whip. The gate guard pointed at him. "Hey! None of that!" he shouted, "Unless you brought enough for everybody!" The miscreant trying to hide the crime, the hand moved swiftly behind his back. The gate guard straightened before resuming his speech.

"I'm gonna go through this again. This is what the horn sounds like." He held the mouthpiece to his lips, screwed up his face, and blew. As it had last time, the horn bellowed in a rich, deep tone, starting out low and stepping up an octave. The sound charged the sky, those closest wincing with its passage. Traffic stopped in the street with rubberneck curiosity. And all at once, the note ended.

After a brief gasp, he panted at the half dozen drivers. "There pant pant now. pant pant What does pant pant that mean?"

There was silence save for the gate guard's huffs and puffs, which were gradually getting further apart.

"...Well?"

A half-dozen-dozen eyes stared blankly at him.

"Hey! Open the gates!" came a cry from the other side of the wall. "Where you at!"

Curses, which won't be translated here, spewed forth from the gate guard as he turned and ran to the stairs. He called to his driving team, "Stand ready, you wall-eyed mongrels!"

Some time after the cry, the gate guard reached the top. Looking down, he saw the source of the call to action. It was a Marrowcrack and what looked like a young Skullcrusher. They each seemed to be carrying something slung over their shoulders. "Who that be?" he called down.

"It's me you idiot, you maggoty boil-ridden slime! Open the gate!"

The guard grumbled and reached for the horn. He missed. Absent-mindedly, he missed again. Where was the horn? It wasn't on its ceremonial stand.

"Uhhh..."

He realized he'd left it downstairs. He called down to the pair, "Hold on!" and made for the stairs again.

Curses came up from the Marrowcrack, but the Skullcrusher remained silent.

"Does that mean we need to open the gates, sire?" one of the drivers asked as the gate guard jumped off the last step and searched for the horn.

"No! Listen for the horn! They don't tell you to open the gates, I do!" He had to stay consistent with them or else it would all fall apart.

Just then, the horn sounded. The gate guard hadn't found it, but it was sounding nonetheless. He looked around. It was almost impossible to triangulate. The sound filled all available space. Then he spotted it.

One of the drivers, the nose-picker, had it and was blowing into it. The gate guard ran and snatched it from him. Sparing no time for curses or punishment, he rushed the stairs again. Halfway up, the walls rumbled.

"No! Not yet! Only go when I blow the horn! Me!" he cried. But it was too late. They had heard the horn, and they had heard him telling them to listen for the horn, so they were already moving their teams and opening the doors before he could get back up to the top and do it properly.

****

Penelope and the Marrowcrack had been running all morning, through midday, and now had reached the walls by evening. She had Salander slung on her back and the Marrowcrack had Chicken, and they were almost out of the supply of water they had scavenged from the kobold camp. After the force of his hurled curses opened the gates, the Marrowcrack wasted no time in entering the city. Penelope drudged after him, her stores of energy finally flagging.

"I don't want to waste a single moment with that useless, incompetent Bloodboil in charge," he was muttering half to himself, "but I'll be blasted by Ogg if that moron got the praise from Lord Kairon for capturing a magical whatsit."

Penelope fell behind, staggered by the size of the walls, the immensity of the doors, and the magnitude of the living quarters in the city. Behind her, the gate guard was hurling obscenities at the drivers and preparing for another on-the-job training session.

Salander, who was unconscious for the journey, now reacted to her slowed pace, groaning. His arms were tied together and looped over her head. She was wearing him like a cloak, and had been since morning. He wasn't able to take in the sights at the moment, and Penelope thought, Chicken was even worse off. She picked up the pace to follow the Marrowcrack.

Chicken, she said silently, I may be getting us in over our heads.

****

The heads of state of the city of Hurraggh were meeting, as they have been increasingly doing, over an expanse of food. Laid out on a long table in the center of the room was an array of trussed bird, roasted pigbeast, select cuts of herdbeast flank, crispy lizard skewers, jellied eyes, minced gizzards, chitlins, candied locust... It was enough to distract even the most starry-eyed and dedicated greenhorn officiate from legal matters in favor of having someone pass them some mustard and that bowl of interesting-looking finger sausages. That is to say, the chiefs of Hurraggh had nary a chance of holding out, and all were eagerly tucking in, setting aside things like integrating formerly hostile peoples comfortably under a single governing body. Kairon sat at the helm of the table, no food in front of him, patiently waiting for the hungry storm to pass so he may pick through the tatters and steer their precious vessel into the harbor of peaceful productivity.

Chief Marrowcrack elbowed Chief Boldbreak beside him.

"Look at him," he said in a gruff whisper, "You ever seen a dark lord sit in a throne?"

Boldbreak grunted. "Never seen any other dark lord but myself."

Marrowcrack rolled his eyes. "Have you ever sat in a throne like that before, then?"

"Yeah. I had a nice big throne. Ivory and leather. Your great great grandparents helped make it, I think."

"No no-..." Merrowcrack began. The comment about his grandparents knocked him off guard. "No Marrowcrack would've helped you make your throne. What are you getting on about?"

"They were an important part. You could say my ancestors leaned heavily on them through the generations." He smirked and sucked meat juice off his thumb.

Marrowcrack studied him in silence for a minute, his brow furrowed, anger welling slowly.

"Their skulls made good arm rests," Boldbreak clarified.

"What I meant to say," Marrowcrack growled with exorbitant patience, "was that he's only sitting. He's not lounging. He's not brooding. You ever just sat on your-" He cut himself off before he mentioned the accursed Boldbreak throne. "You ever just sat when you were presiding over your underlings?"

And Boldbreak, now pulled from the topic of his throne, considered their lord seriously. Lord Kairon was, in fact, a humble leader. As regal as a medical exam office. As lordly as a library.

Boldbreak screwed his face up in consideration. "So, what does that mean for us?"

An attendant approached the throne, sending an instinctive hush down the table. She carried a simple bowl, and when she reached the throne Kairon looked at her as though snapping from a daydream.

"Whassat?" Boldbreak whispered to Marrowcrack.

In answer, Marrowcrack stood up. To Lord Kairon he boomed, "My Lord, as per your request, we have procured the fruits of the oasis." He stressed the unfamiliar word – fruits – testing it out. "The alternative food source to the flesh of beasts. These figs and dates we present to you."

Kairon plucked one courteously from the bowl, the kindness of the gesture making the attendant flinch. He studied it against the light, holding it between his thumb and forefinger.

"Wonderful, Chief Marrowcrack. Our diet consists too heavily of meat and fats," he made a sweeping gesture with his other hand indicating the food which populated the table. He replaced the fig in the bowl. "We can begin growing our food from the ground for increased sustainability and a more robust foundation. I would like to incorporate these fruits in our farming strategy."

To one of the other chieftains he said, "Chief Sharpteeth, are you prepared to report on the farming initiative?"

She coughed and spluttered into her wine, having just at that moment decided to take a sip. Beating on her chest to clear her throat, she said, "Plots have been dispersed among the commoners. There is little land here in the wastes which suit your requirements, however. The land around the oases grows sparse as the water disappears."

He considered her words while sitting utterly still. He made no contemplative gesture, and gave the impression that the words had been thrown down a well. The table waited for the splash.

"If it would please you, Lord," Marrowcrack said, "try one of the fruits?"

He looked to the speaker, again as though coming out of sleep. "Hmm? Oh, no. No, no thank you." He politely waved off the attendant. As she passed by Marrowcrack, he made a curt gesture. She would dispose of the fruits in the pile just out of sight of town hall reserved for the things Lord Kairon rejected.

Slowly Kairon said, "I have been working on a solution." He looked at Sharpteeth. "It may only be temporary, as it is dangerous to employ, but it has become increasingly necessary for our goals."

With a meaningful look, he summoned an attendant who brought forth a small clay jar. It was handmade, though eerily precise in its craftorcship, and looked no larger than a fist. Kairon took it in hand and displayed it for all to see.

"I will not explain it, but I can demonstrate it for you. Empty your cups and pass them to me." In a matter of moments, a battalion of goblets sat near to him on the table. Carefully, he filled one cup from the container. It brimmed with clear water, and Kairon passed it back.

He then did this with another cup. And another. And another.

The chieftains watched on as many times the amount of what the container could hold was poured into their glasses and the glasses returned to them.

Marrowcrack looked into his. It didn't look like proper water. It was lacking the silt and tiny worms. He watched Boldbreak stick a tongue into the liquid.

"It don't taste like anything," he reported. "But there's a lot of it to go around. And it all fits in that tiny jug?"

Kairon held up his invention now that every cup was full. He looked at another attendant, who ushered a team of goblins carrying a much larger pot, which they set on the ground next to him. It came up to his shoulder. He tipped the pot over and held it as water rushed forth endlessly into the tall basin.

"The water in this container is limitless, pure, and portable. With this invention, I believe we can overcome the issues we face on the farming front." This he spoke over the sound of the water being perpetually emptied into the much larger container. The orcs seated at the table watched on.

Marrowcrack was the first to speak up, "Lord, if I may-" but he was cut off by Sharpteeth. "There is but one of these devices! How can you say this will benefit all of Hurraggh?"

"It's infinite water!" Boldbreak argued. "We can have as much as we need!"

"Infinite maybe. But look how slowly it comes out. The tall jug has barely filled at all. And how do we get these to the plots quickly enough to wet the ground?" She hurled a bowl at him along with her rebuttal.

Candied locusts and shards of pottery exploded off his face, and he picked up the femur he had been chewing on. He brandished it like a club, and his

"They'll get my water when I'm good and ready to give it to them." He said it slowly, emphasizing the words.

Marrowcrack shoved Boldbreak on the shoulder. "Your water? Your water?"

They both stood up quickly, their chairs shrieking as they slid over the floor, and they stood chest to chest.

"Yeah, my water," he huffed.

Marrowcrack was about to accuse the Boldbreak of the slaying of his ancestors when a pounding came from the head of the table.

"I demand order," Kairon said loudly but gently. "Stand down this instant."

A conflicting look overcame Boldbreak, and the two broke eye contact at the same time. Boldbreak dropped his bone club on the table and righted his chair. Marrowcrack did the same with his chair, and they both sat down again.

They looked to their leader for further instructions, but a guard had entered and was whispering in his ear.

To the table, Kairon said, "I will leave you to your meal. Please excuse me." He followed the guard out of the dining hall, bringing the magical water container with him.

In the antechamber, a Merrowcrack and a Skullcrush awaited an audience. Kairon bade the two to enter.

The Marrowcrack had told Penelope to put the kobolds on their feet, then gruffly tried to revive them with some refreshments brought by one of the servants. Chicken and Salander groggily tried to work feeling back into their arms. Penelope had tried to argue for more stops along the way to the city, but the Marrowcrack had just told her to give the two some water while they ran. Stopping wasn't an option.

"Ah, Rigorous, I see you've returned. I hope you had a fruitful excursion." Kairon said mirthfully. "I don't recognize these faces. Please, tell me your news."

"My Lord," the Marrowcrack said, saluting. Kairon sighed audibly, but made no comment.

"While I and Wildmere the Bloodboil were on patrol, sire, we came across two individuals of the lesser races."

Kairon glanced at the downtrodden kobolds, to which Rigorous said, "Not these two, sire. The other two were killed for sport."

Penelope withheld her surprise. Chicken was too tired to register the comment, but Salander suddenly looked sicker.

"Before we slaughtered them, sire, they told us of an orc, which I and the Bloodboil have since learned was taking the rite of the nameless god."

Here Kairon tutted, "Heathen ritual. I thought we sorted all of that out by now."

Penelope spoke up, saying, "Sire, I have been away many months performing the rite. I was hitherto unaware of the change of command. I am a Skullcrusher, sire."

"Well, young lady, I think I can forgive this only once," he said sternly, "We only follow the two true gods, Neos and Deos. With your tribe now a part of this city, I expect you to conform to civilized society. I hope you will familiarize yourself with our priests in your own time."

Penelope didn't know what that meant but figured a "yes, sire" was in order.

"Please, continue Rigorous. I feel you have more to tell me."

Rigorous also enacted a "yes, sire" and continued, "The two killed for sport had indicated an area not far from our patrol where the wayward orc resided, sire. When we went to inspect, we came upon a tribe of lesser races like the ones which came to us, as well as this Skullcrusher here, sire."

"And what did you do with them, pray?"

"Sire, we took the leader," indicating Salander, "and while sub-jugating the tribe we encountered a….magical individual." He tugged on Chicken's leash, bringing him forward.

"Another one? It's only been a week since Justafar brought me the previous one. Kudos, Rigorous, and well done." His tone implied a golf clap, which was offputting for the Marrowcrack. On one hand he recognized the praise, but on the other it didn't feel like enough. He ripped off another "yes, sire."

"Tell me, Rigorous, though I think I know the answer. What do you and Wildmere plan to do from here? I assume he is with the…tribe of lesser races? No, actually, please tell me about these creatures first."

Rigorous only looked puzzled, so Penelope took the initiative, saying, "These are kobolds, sire."

"Kobolds?" he said, trying out the word. "The magical being brought to me by Justafar had been mistaken for a goblin, but was in fact a gnome. We seem to not make the distinction between these lesser races." He noted the puzzlement which Rigorous had just wiped off his face. "I have never before heard of kobolds. You, Skullcrusher. You seem to be knowledgeable in the area. When this meeting is over, please stay, as I would like you to instruct me to the best of your ability. Do you have more for me, Rigorous?"

"No, sire," said the Marrowcrack, perturbed by the special treat-ment given to this upstart. "Just, if I may sire," he said, remembering himself, "I would like to take more orcs with me on the return trip."

Kairon signaled and two attendants detached themselves from the wall. "Please take it up with Spinewrack and Krarl out in the antechamber. Thank you, Rigorous."

Kairon had kept Penelope in his gaze for the entirety of his last comment.

www.ingramcontent.com/pod-product-compliance
Lightning Source LLC
Chambersburg PA
CBHW071019180726
48291CB00004B/1539